Y0-CAS-363

Kally Hawenstein

Thank you for being a great student and achieving the highest grade (99.19%) in my class Econ 2.02.02 (Fall 14)

Nand

Journey

NAND ARORA

Copyright © 2013 Nand Arora

All rights reserved.

ISBN-10: 1484931254
ISBN-13: 978-1484931257

DEDICATION

This book is dedicated to my wonderful family.
My wife Madhu, our daughter Namita, and our son Rohan.
Thank you for being a great family.
I love you all.

INSPIRATION FOR THIS BOOK

This book is dedicated to:

Late Janpeet Singh (Cherry)
December 22, 2006 – August 09, 2011

You will never be forgotten. Your death will not go in vain.

Almost two years ago, I read a story and saw a picture of a small Sikh child with big, bright eyes who was crushed under the wheels of his school bus, in New Delhi, and I cried. Janpeet Singh was only four years old at that time.

His death, unfortunately, is not unusual. India leads the world in traffic fatalities, and a startling number of them involve schoolchildren. Buses crash, careen down embankments, and topple into gorges. All too often in India, such accidents are shrugged off with a fatalistic attitude.

That's when I knew I had to do something, or else I would have regret and guilt forever.

On the day Janpeet Singh died, his father dressed him neatly in his crisp school uniform for picture day at his nursery school. At school, Janpeet, the four-year old, smiled shyly for the camera. But he never made it home.

That afternoon, when Janpeet's grandfather arrived to pick him up at the bus stop, he found him lying on the roadside in a pool of blood. Janpeet's schoolbooks were scattered on the ground, and his eight-year old brother, Parmeet, was kneeling beside Janpeet's crumpled body, shaking him.

"Get up, Cherry!" Parmeet implored, calling his brother by his nickname. "Get up!"

CREDIT

I consider myself a visionary, but not a master of all subjects. I envisioned this story and how I wanted it to be perceived. In that sense it is original work. But I am not a psychiatrist, a pilot or even a good writer. I don't claim to know everything about mental illnesses, planes, pilots or even writing a good novel. Therefore, everything in this book is not all my own work. Considering the subject matter, it hardly could be. Rather, it has resulted from my extensive research into the work of many specialists in those areas. I am grateful for their work, and I have cited their work at the end of the novel under notes by each chapter.

EDITORS

Sue Skiendziel

Rohan Arora

Special thanks to two of the best editors in the world. My friend and colleague, Ms. Sue Skiendziel, who teaches English at Jackson Community College, and Rohan Arora, my son and a freshman at the University of Michigan. I would not have been able to finish this book without their help and inspiration.

ACKNOWLEDGMENTS

SPECIAL THANKS TO THE FOLLOWING REVIEWERS
FOR THEIR TIMELY, AND CONSTRUCTIVE
FFEDBACK THAT MADE THIS NOVEL POSSIBLE...

Sue Skiendziel – Editor

Rohan Arora – Editor

Stephanie Davis

Dr. Sadhana Alangar

Rahul Krishnan

Nikki Krishnan

Mark Kramer

Jane Kramer

Members of the Book Club of Jackson

Amber Burkhart

Autumn Rose Wood

Charlotte Coulston

Cindi Parker

Coralie Johnson

Devlin Giroux

Leah Denda

Patricia McClaffin

CONTENTS

ACKNOWLEDGMENTS

Special thanks to Ashwati Matthew and Jakob McCaskey in helping me start this novel by lending their outstanding writing skills that were used in part in chapters 1 and 2 respectively.

01 - DARKNESS FALLS

MAIN CHARACTERS IN THE BOOK

Akash – Protagonist

Aarti – Akash's wife

Shreya – Akash's daughter

Rohit – Akash's son

Parvati (Jhai ji, Grandma, Daadi Ma) – Akash's mother

With sirens blaring at full throttle and lights flashing, the ambulance threaded through the streets of Ann Arbor to the E.R. at the University of Michigan Medical Center with urgency. EMTs pushed through the swinging doors with precision, and befitting efficacy with Akash strapped to a gurney. The E.R. was as busy as a beehive, with a motley of people darting about—physicians, residents, nurses, technicians, patients, family members, EMTs, and police. It was surprising how calm and relaxed everyone seemed despite this buzz of activity. Aarti and

Rakesh followed the E.M.T. to the front desk.

"Patient's name?" the nurse asked as she registered Akash, while another nurse checked his vital signs. "Has this ever happened before?"

"Yes," replied Akash with faint voice.

"Allergies?"

"No."

"Shortness of breath?"

"Yes."

"Dizziness?"

"Yes."

"Pain?"

"Yes."

"Recreational drugs?"

"No."

"Do you smoke?"

"No."

"Name of your primary care physician?"

"Dr. Paul Davis."

"Has he been informed of the situation yet?"

"No, but I'll call him right now," replied Aarti, after completing the required paperwork. She then quickly called Akash's psychiatrist, Dr. Johnson, and the family's primary care physician, Dr. Davis, and updated them on what had happened.

Electronic noises filled acoustic niches in the E.R. with beeping wall monitors, ringing phones, printers spitting out EKGs, beepers going off, loud pages over the intercom as nurses continue their work unfazed and move Akash's gurney to the major multipurpose (MAMP) bed for the doctor on duty for an MRI and other more complex tests.

With most vital signs normal thus far and awaiting the doctor on duty for further examination, Aarti and Rakesh felt a sigh of relief and informed everyone at home of the situation. Parvati and the children were just as delighted and thanked God for listening to their prayers and could not wait until the next morning for a complete update. Aarti also thanked Rakesh for all his help and support and promised to keep him updated as he prepared to leave for the night.

Adorned with a glittering gold necklace, bangles, and a brightly colored traditional Indian *sari*, which was elaborately swathed around her body, Aarti sat alone in the E.R. waiting area. Her mind wandered restlessly from one thought to another as she tried to figure out the cause of Akash's devastating anxiety attack earlier that evening. She carefully analyzed the day's events in her mind, but everything seemed so normal and so festive.

The whole family had taken a day off to celebrate *Diwali* as they did every year. The auspicious day had started beautifully with Akash and the children decorating the whole house inside and out with festive lights and Aarti preparing traditional Indian sweets and dishes. Parvati narrated the story of Diwali for the children, a ritual celebrated in their family, followed by worship in the temple. "Nothing seemed to be out of the ordinary. Nothing at all," thought Aarti as she rubbed her forehead and was immersed in deep thoughts trying to find clues.

"Then, what? Could it be that Akash was overly concerned about the evening's presentation on stage?" She thought aloud in her mind but quickly ruled that possibility out, because Akash and both young, teenage children were so excited. They had been rehearsing their songs for days. Akash loved teaching the children about their heritage and culture. He loved showcasing them at every cultural event. She thought about how they had arrived that evening at Washtenaw Community College's auditorium to celebrate Diwali. Children, dressed in an array of colors, laughing and playing; women, dressed in delicately woven saris, singing joyously; men, smiling and preparing to recite the *mantras* welcomed them as they arrived in the auditorium. The lights shimmered, showcasing a time of pure spiritual reawakening. The whole auditorium was decorated with hundreds of *diyas*. Diwali reminded celebrators to eliminate the negative aura and to bring in the positive energy and ignite their inner spiritual light. Children of all ages participated in a variety of songs and ethnic folk dances which were as diverse and as colorful as India, its people, and its culture. One group after another performed to loud applause from the audience.

Akash appeared calm and confident when he arrived on stage, accompanied by Shreya and Rohit to present their selections. They had chosen each song and dance routine carefully so as to ensure that the meaning of Diwali was not mistranslated by a single soul in that auditorium. For the first song, the family wanted to ensure the optimistic energy was sustained for the entire evening. Dressed in a white *kurta*, Akash symbolized the purity, or simply, the purification of the human soul; Shreya, dressed in a glimmering red and gold *lehenga*, beamed brightly as she brought her palms together and bowed benevolently. She was accompanied by her brother Rohit, also dressed in a traditional, white Indian kurta.

Akash and Aarti's minds connected, and eyes smiled as they cherished this moment as proud Indian parents.

Although Akash, Shreya, and Rohit were the only three forces on the stage, when they began to sing the first verse, their voices echoed in unison through the walls of the illuminated auditorium; the feeling sent chills through Aarti's body as she felt the packed auditorium of about 200 patrons singing along with joy.

Mere Tumhare, Sabke Liye... Happy Diwali
Saare Sitaarein, Uske Liye... Happy Diwali
Usne Banayi, Sabke Liye... Happy Diwali
Meaning...

It is for me, for you, and for everyone... Happy Diwali
All the stars are for him... Happy Diwali
He made it for everyone... Happy Diwali

Akash's mother, Parvati, clapped her hands to the rhythmic tune of the song, as she sang along lightly with her family. She thought of her late husband and how he would have enjoyed this song and would have been so proud of his grandchildren. Her eyes began to fill with tears, but she brushed them aside and reminded herself to focus on the positive attributes of the moment.

Singing, dancing, clapping, excitement, and positive energy, continued in the auditorium for people of all ages and places which embodied the spirit of community, free from all barriers and prejudices until the unexpected happened.

Aarti's eyes welled up and her muscles became tensed as she thought of what happened next on stage.

Time stood still for Akash.

The Diwali celebration's cheerfulness contrasted with the dreaded darkness that engulfed Akash's mind. First faintly, and then with force, the images filled Akash with fear and anxiety. Sharp, shooting pains flooded Akash's mind sporadically and vigorously like the monsoons of India.

Akash grabbed his head as if to hold the heaviness he felt within. Shreya screamed in fright as Rohit reached out for his father.

The sweat poured profusely through his pores as Akash clenched his forehead tighter, his knuckles grew whiter. But the timing and severity could not have been worse than right in the middle of a performance with his family on stage on this most auspicious day of Diwali.

Akash couldn't bear the weight any longer and plummeted to the floor.

The luminous ceremony was brought to a halt, as Aarti and Parvati rushed to Akash. Aarti felt faint, but she knew she had to be strong for her family.

People in the auditorium stood in shock, perplexed over what to do with the unexpected situation on stage. Darkness engulfed the celebratory spirits in the whole auditorium as if the Hindu Goddess *Kali* had overshadowed Lord *Rama's* victory over demon *Ravana*.

Some of the men gathered around the stage. Two of them held Shreya and Rohit from falling.

Her heart in pain, Aarti called her husband's name, "Akash." As they once heard the lovely voices of the Kumar family, every soul in that auditorium felt the love and panic in her voice. The auspicious occasion was unbalanced by the misfortune of Akash's fall. The luminous ceremony brought misfortune to the Kumar family.

The noise of the sirens grew stronger and stronger, overwhelming the fainting sounds of the celebration in the auditorium.

Members of the EMT team rushed to the scene of the fall. The male paramedic asked Aarti, "Ma'am can you tell us what happened?" Her face grew pale, and her eyes produced a blank stare. Rakesh, a close friend in the auditorium, told the EMT about the incident. The male paramedic checked Akash's vital signs and told the female EMT to check Aarti's. Two other paramedics arrived to the scene with a stretcher. The first paramedic, along with the new arrivals, lifted Akash's body with a count of three onto the stretcher.

At that moment, Aarti's body sprang to life as she said, "I want to be with my husband." The female paramedic helped Aarti up, and with great effort, Aarti pulled her feet together and stood erect. She ran to her husband's side, grasped his hand, and shut her eyes as the tears trickled down her face and she whispered something softly.

Rakesh informed the paramedics that he was a close friend of the family and wanted to ride along with them as well. Aarti nodded her head in agreement. Rakesh turned to one of his friends in the auditorium and told him to look after the remaining members of the Kumar family.

The paramedics pushed the stretcher as Aarti clung tightly to her husband, and Rakesh followed closely behind.

"This is the second serious attack in the last two months," thought Aarti. "What could it be?" She struggled to find reasons behind such severe attacks all night in the E.R. waiting area in vain. She wished that she had specialized in psychiatry instead of rheumatology so that she could help Akash.

Her thoughts were interrupted suddenly by the sound of her beeper early in the morning. It was the E.R. doctor asking her to sign Akash's release papers.

Though Aarti was quite used to hectic schedules and long nights at the hospital as a physician, the night as a wife whose husband was in the E.R. was longer, more arduous, and more painful than any other she had experienced before. Aarti felt humbled and felt this was a priceless experience, though not a desired one.

****

02 DR. ROBERT JOHNSON

The overcast sky hung with a grey haze that morning as Akash and Aarti pulled into the clean concrete driveway of their suburban home. While the grass still held its hue of green, the orange glow of the sun hid away, as colorless light shone down on the landscape and painted the somber mood of the two. It had been a relatively short trip home from the hospital where Akash had spent the night in observation, and the two said few words as sadness filled their hearts. Aarti steered the SUV across the driveway, put the car into park, and turned off the ignition. Their silence was heightened without the hum of the car's engine. Aarti looked over to Akash, drew a breath, and broke the silence. "Are you feeling any better?" she pried. The silence resumed for a moment; then Akash laboriously sighed and concluded, "a bit" in a low voice. Slowly Akash turned his gaze upon his wife who looked worriedly and lovingly upon him. Her dark hair and pretty face were not enough to hide the weariness in her eyes from the night she spent awake at the hospital. Aarti watched Akash and analyzed the troubling expression in his eyes that stared back at her through a medicated haze.

"You seem calmer," Aarti commented hopefully but with thinly veiled reservations. Akash paused, and then looked out the passenger window to the side of the brick suburban home they had shared for years. The lawn was meticulously kept as not a blade of grass was out of place, except for randomly blowing leaves. Off to the side of the house, leading to the backyard, a spigot hung from the concrete foundation. Loosely connected to the spigot, a brightly colored green garden hose descended down from the threaded mouth and coiled next to the sidewalk like a serpent, as the water slowly dripped from the coupling above. Akash stared longingly and whimsically, wishing to see Lord *Vishnu* appear atop of *Sheshnag* so he could plead to him for help. The spigot continued to drip.

"Let's go inside," Akash decided aloud, and the two opened their doors to the chilly breeze outside. They made their way through the garage and into the house where Parvati greeted them anxiously with the soft, soothing sounds of *bhajans* playing in the background. Both Akash and Aarti bowed and touched Parvati's feet in a customary fashion to show their respect and receive her blessings.

With her hands on their heads, Parvati gently leaned over and kissed their foreheads in her kind, gentle, and distinguished manner.

"May God bless you with a long, happy life together," she uttered in her soft spoken voice.

"How are you feeling, *beta?*" she asked, turning to Akash with tears in her eyes.

"I am feeling fine, Jhai ji," replied Akash, holding back his pain.

"Come inside," she gently guided them inside, holding Akash's hand.

The modern kitchen was welcoming to Akash. The kitchen was clean and well-kept as its marble countertop held nothing atop but its characteristic gloss. Akash directly made his way to the family room and heavily sat down upon the wood trimmed leather sofa. The large room was tastefully decorated with brass light fixtures and wooden trim. The curtains were only slightly ajar, letting just a little of the grey exterior light into the room which was encompassed by shadows. The room was largely silent until Aarti and Parvati entered a few moments later.

"Why don't you both freshen up while I fix breakfast for you?" suggested Parvati lovingly. "You will feel better." Parvati paused for a moment and then returned to the kitchen and began the soft clamors that food preparation entailed. In the kitchen, Parvati nobly sought to work away the distress of the previous night by cooking. Normally one of her favorite pastimes, she struggled to find the happiness that usually welled up inside her. She quietly and delicately started to cook the breakfast and set up the table while waiting for Akash and Aarti to join her as the warm, spicy, and inviting aroma of cooking filled the kitchen.

"How are you feeling now?" asked Parvati while pouring tea at the breakfast table.

"Little sore," Akash replied, pointing to his head.

"How are the children doing?" asked Akash, as he tried to steer the conversation.

"They both truly missed you. They were worried last night and did not want to go to school this morning, but I sent them off anyway," replied Parvati.

"Good."

"What did the doctors say?"

"Not much, really; they treated wounds suffered from the fall and kept me for observation overnight."

"So, what's next?" inquired Parvati, looking at Akash and Aarti.

"I have already called our family doctor and updated him on everything. I have also set up an appointment with Dr. Johnson at 4:00 p.m. this afternoon so that we can meet Shreya and Rohit before leaving," replied Aarti.

"I think you are making too much of this incidence," said Akash, putting on a bold face.

"I don't think so, Akash. It is not normal to have such a severe anxiety attacks one after another. And I don't mean it only as a loving wife, but also as being a doctor myself," she said with seriousness on her face and confidence in her voice, as Parvati nodded in agreement.

"I think both of you should take some rest before the children get back and you have to go to see Dr. Johnson," interrupted Parvati wisely, so as to cut short any further disagreements while clearing the dishes from the table.

Akash lumbered up the stairs to his bedroom for a nap. Akash's sleep was fitful. The darkened room hid him in shadows as he rested underneath a dark blue comforter. His brow glistened with sweat and his body occasionally twitched as he dreamt. His eyes were in rapid movement beneath their lids while his mind jumped and danced from image to image. In the dream, Akash struggled along a mountain trail barely wide enough to walk on. Its reddish brown path separated him from its sparse vegetation and rocky terrain to his sides. Onward he stumbled, further up the steep path as it wound back and forth taking residence in any spot that a foothold could be held. The sky above him shone in a cloudy grey haze that descended upon him, constricting his vision. The trees grew thinner and thinner as he grew shorter and shorter in breath. The nip of cold snapped at him from each side like a wild dog as he feverishly struggled with greater and greater urgency up the mountain. In minutes that seemed like hours, Akash's legs buckled, and he fell to the ground. A weight was upon his back that was simply too great for him, and he could move no further. He lay there next to the black granite and amongst the moist crimson dirt, panting, struggling to breathe. Seconds passed as his breathing grew constrained, and in a brief moment of consciousness he thought, "This is it, this is the end." The granite to his right sat motionless, wise, and silent.

Akash awoke, startled, with a racing heartbeat. The dream's real and starkly frightening nature worried him as he ripped the covers off his body and sat on the edge of the plush bed. He rested his head in his hands as he sighed deeply, regaining his breath as reality greeted him coldly. "Why is this happening to me?" Akash thought, mournfully. He then rose from the bed, approached the curtains, and opened them to reveal the familiar and calming view of the lake.

Akash's thoughts were cheerily interrupted with the chime of the doorbell. For a moment, he felt the heavens had descended upon him as he knew Shreya and Rohit had arrived from school. He made his way down the winding stairway slowly to greet them.

"Papa!" the children screamed with joy, as they showered Akash with hugs and kisses.

"How are you, Papa?" asked Shreya with tears in her eyes.

"Happiest man on earth, beta," he replied with a grin while hugging and holding back his pain.

"How was your day at school?"

"It was good, but we were worried about you all day," both replied. They took their shoes off at the door and Parvati set the table with milk and snacks.

Everyone sat together at the kitchen table while Shreya and Rohit gulped down the milk impatiently.

"Slow down, guys," chided Aarti with a smile on her face. Everyone broke into laughter.

"Don't forget your appointment," Parvati reminded Akash.

"What appointment?" interrupted the children with a worried look on their faces.

"Your dad has to go and see Dr. Johnson. We won't be long," replied Aarti.

"Is it about last night?" asked Shreya, as everyone's disposition turned somber.

Parvati swiftly got out of her chair and quickly guided Akash and Aarti towards the door in an effort to steer the topic off the conversation into something more cheerful.

"We will wait for you for dinner," said Parvati.

"See you soon," said Aarti, as they both waved, pulling their SUV away from the house.

**

"Sorry you had to go through so much last night at the hospital because of me," said Akash graciously looking at Aarti, interrupting the humming sound of the engine.

"You would have done the same for me if I needed you," replied Aarti. "Isn't that what being together means in life?" She continued while Akash nodded reluctantly in agreement.

"I know, but I still wish the incident had not happened. Everyone was enjoying the Diwali celebrations," Akash sighed in a melancholic tone.

"I understand how you feel Akash, but it is not something you brought onto yourself," reflected Aarti wistfully.

"Sometimes I wonder if in fact I actually do bring it

upon myself," said Akash.

"What do you mean?" asked Aarti with a blank look on her face.

Their conversation was cut short as Aarti pulled into the behavioral health's outpatient department parking lot at the University of Michigan hospital, a short distance from their home.

"Hello!" Lisa welcomed them both with a smile as they arrived at the office.

"Please have a seat; Dr. Johnson will be right with you."

Akash and Aarti did not need any introduction because both were quite familiar to the entire staff at the office, not only because Akash was a patient there, but also because Aarti worked as a rheumatologist at the same hospital.

Akash and Aarti waited silently in the lounge, each turning magazine pages while soft, soothing music played in the background. The eerie silence in the room was soon interrupted with the familiar welcoming sound of Dr. Johnson as he arrived to receive Akash.

"Hello, Akash! Please come in," invited Dr. Johnson with a smile, putting his arm around Akash's shoulder while waving at Aarti. Dr. Johnson was a psychiatrist in his 50's with gray hair, blue eyes, and deep horizontal lines across his forehead, and yawning crevices between his brows. He had been Akash's psychiatrist for more than fifteen years and was a good friend of the family.

"How are you feeling now?" the doctor inquired as he pointed Akash towards the chair to be seated.

"Much better," replied Akash, taking his seat across from the doctor.

"So tell me what happened."

Akash shrugged his shoulders a bit and shook his head. Akash then began reciting his painful tale about his panic stricken state at the Diwali function. The doctor's face turned serious. The story continued for nearly half an hour as the doctor frequently interrupted with probing questions, and Akash did his best to provide all the details he could of his fragile inner psyche.

"Oh, that's so unfortunate," the doctor said sympathetically after Akash finished describing the incidence.

"How are your wife and family handling all of this?"

"They have been particularly caring and supportive, but also very worried about me."

"I can imagine because that was quite a difficult experience for everyone involved, including you," the doctor empathized.

"Akash, is there anything different that happened recently that may have caused this anxiety attack? This is the second time it has happened during the last two months," the doctor probed after a short pause.

"Not that I can think of," replied Akash.

"Are you taking your medication on a regular basis?"

"Yes, I am."

The doctor thought pensively for nearly a minute. His greying hair and lanky figure added to the seriousness in his eyes.

Akash's anticipation deepened as the genuinely caring and confident doctor pondered.

Suddenly, the doctor turned to Akash and asked, "Is it

alright if I invite Aarti in on the conversation?"

"I guess so," replied Akash with some reservation.

Soon, the doctor returned to his office, accompanied by Aarti, and continued with his prognosis.

"Akash, I have known you for more than fifteen years now; you are like family to me and I care about you deeply. We have been able to manage your illness for the most part with the help of medications and cognitive-behavioral therapy, but I am just as perplexed and shocked as you are with your recent, debilitating anxiety attacks. Your illness is truly a stubborn one, and honestly, it has been a struggle to make much more progress than we already have against it. I could change medication and adjust doses, but we have already been through all of that." He paused for a moment; finally Dr. Johnson stood up and said something completely unexpected. "I am going to refer you to Dr. Kiran Joshi for treatment."

For a moment, there was a distressing silence in the room as Aarti and Akash absorbed this startling announcement. Many questions darted through Akash and Aarti's minds. Aarti was somewhat familiar with Dr. Joshi's name and had heard rumors of her controversial medical practices in her inner circle of professional friends.

Shocked and perplexed, Akash sat with no emotions on his face as if he had already accepted Dr. Johnson's decision as another prescription. Aarti, however, was not satisfied with the decision. She wanted to know more about the reasons behind Dr. Johnson's decision and about Dr. Joshi and how it might affect Akash in the short-run and in the long-run.

Dr. Johnson went on to tell them about Dr. Kiran Joshi, a psychiatrist in her early 40's who had her own practice in town. "I have personally known Dr. Joshi for almost five years now; she is a smart, articulate, effective doctor, and a graduate of Stanford Medical School," he continued, confidently.

"What about the investigations and accusations swirling around her practice?" interrupted Aarti.

"Right," responded Dr. Johnson in a matter-of-fact tone as if he had already thought about that question coming up. "I don't buy that for a minute. Just because she is being investigated does not mean she is guilty, and just because her methods are controversial does not mean that they are ineffective," he added candidly. "You see, each of us tends to think we see things as they are; that we are objective. But this is not the case. We see the world, not as it is, but as we are – or as we are conditioned to see it. That's what makes it controversial until we have what I call the 'Aha!' experience when someone finally 'sees' the picture in another way -- a shift in paradigm."

Akash and Aarti had never witnessed Dr. Johnson speak as passionately before. His eyes were sparkling, and his expressions were animated as he continued in support of Dr. Joshi.

"But we have established medical ethics to guide us," interrupted Aarti.

"Yes, we have," Dr. Johnson concurred. "But remember the physician's oath? 'The health of my patient will be my number one consideration,'" he exhorted.

"Until the germ theory was developed, a high percentage of women and children died during childbirth, and no one could understand why. In military skirmishes, more men were dying from small wounds and diseases than from the major traumas on the front lines. But as soon as the germ theory was developed, a whole new paradigm, a better, improved way of understanding what was happening made dramatic, significant medical improvement possible," he sermonized in a scholarly voice.

"The United States today is the fruit of a paradigm shift. The traditional concept of government for centuries had been a monarchy, the divine right of kings. Then a different paradigm was developed – government of the people, by the people, and for the people, and a constitutional democracy was born."

"Look at Gandhi. Though he held no office or political position, through compassion, courage, fasting, moral persuasion, and peaceful insubordination, he eventually brought England to its knees, breaking the political repression of three hundred million Indians and inspiring Nelson Mandela and Dr. Martin Luther King Jr."

"Are you suggesting Dr. Joshi might be up to something so monumental?" asked Aarti.

"No, I am not making any such claims," clarified Dr. Johnson.

"Then what?"

Sensing the hesitation on Aarti's face, Dr. Johnson emphatically added, "As the saying goes, if you always do what you've always done, you'll always get what you always got, and you'll always feel what you always felt. I believe it is time to try a different approach. Besides, being that she hails from the same culture, Dr. Joshi might be in a better position to offer a different perspective into Akash's illness. It certainly cannot hurt to have another opinion. I am certainly not abandoning you; instead, I am looking out for you. I will personally call Dr. Joshi and request that she accept Akash as her patient. I need you to be persistent, however, with Dr. Joshi as she might be reluctant to accept Akash as her patient under the circumstances," concluded Dr. Johnson as he opened his office door while shaking their hands.

"Please continue taking your medication; I will call you tomorrow," he said as he waved.

****

03 THE UNKNOWN

Varying hues of fiery red and yellow colors of the twilight filled the endless sky in defiance of the vanishing sun dipping beneath the horizon as Aarti pulled her SUV from the parking lot.

"So, what did you think of the meeting?" asked Aarti with mixed emotions.

"It was alright."

"Why were you so quiet?"

"Well, what was I supposed to say?"

"What did you think of his decision?"

"It was shocking, to say the least; I wish he had consulted us ahead of time," he confided.

"I have to agree with you on that," replied Aarti, shaking her head in agreement as she drove along the scenic Huron River.

The colors of the sunset spread over the river like a

great big, romantic, inspirational fire in the sky, becoming more beautiful as it died down.

Ignoring the beautiful surroundings, Aarti paused for a minute then asked, "Are you nervous about the situation?"

"I am a little concerned, but not really nervous."

"What are your concerns?" pried Aarti.

"The unknown, I guess."

"You mean Dr. Joshi?" Aarti prodded.

"Well, that and everything else you brought up about the rumors surrounding her practice."

"Well, I just wanted to be sure, because you mean everything to me," replied Aarti as she glanced at Akash with sincerity.

"I know, and you all mean everything to me as well. I wish the incident had never happened," he said, as he looked out the window at the sunset.

"Things happen you know! It's not like you brought it onto yourself."

"Sometimes I wonder if I did," he pondered.

"What do you mean? Don't be so hard on yourself."

"Hey! Can you please pull over for a minute?" he asked Aarti, pointing towards the viewing area along Huron River.

"Sure," replied Aarti, as she gently steered the SUV in the designated parking area off to the side.

Cool, crisp, air surrounded them as they stepped outside along the river.

"Wow! Look at the beautiful colors," said Akash, pointing towards the sky.

"Yes, the colors are so warm, and the intensity of light is just enough to soothe you after a long and hectic day," said Aarti with a smile while holding Akash's hand.

"Yes, indeed," replied Akash as they strolled along the mystically, color soaked water of the river.

"Everything will be alright," assured Aarti, squeezing his hands gently.

"I know," replied Akash, looking into Aarti's eyes lovingly.

"You know, the sunset reminds me of an old friend waving good bye; they are leaving, but you are filled with confidence that you will see them again," he continued, with a poetic voice.

"Thank you for everything you have done for me. I feel safe and secure with you around," he continued as they walked back towards the SUV.

"You are very welcome! I will call Dr. Johnson and get an update tomorrow before I call Dr. Joshi for an appointment," replied Aarti, pulling out on the road.

"Aren't you going to work tomorrow?"

"No, I am taking a few days off until everything is straightened out. I have already called the office and asked them to cancel all my appointments for this week. I'm sure they'll understand."

"It is really not necessary, you know! I can call and make those appointments. I am feeling alright, you know," Akash tried to assure in vain.

"I am sure you can, but this is something I want to do. Being a physician myself, I feel the need to find out what is happening. And being a wife, I am determined to see my husband live and enjoy a life without depression and anxiety."

Disarmed by her love, determination, and affection, Akash sat quietly, holding back his tears of gratitude until they arrived at home.

***

Tucked away at the end of a long winding driveway, surrounded by tall mature trees on a lakefront, the Kumar family's home was gloriously illuminated for perhaps the most well-known of the Indian festivals, Diwali, colloquially known as the festival of lights. Randomly scattered leaves in the yard, reminiscent of the recent autumn that began with a slow dance of turning leaves in broad strokes of colors, had given way to the chilly winds, morning frost, and bare trees as precursors of the winter season. The home drew attention from the people driving on a distant main road, unaware of the tradition, guessing, that perhaps the home was decorated early for Christmas.

The tantalizing spicy aroma of Jhai ji's cooking blended with a sweet dose of hugs from the children greeted Akash and Aarti as they entered the house. The air was redolent of freshly cooked vegetables and spicy mint chutney mixed with fresh coriander.

"How did everything go at the doctor's office?" asked Parvati and the children.

"Everything went well," replied Akash while enjoying the exhilarating aroma of the food.

"Thank God," said Parvati, walking towards the dining room.

"The food smells so nice, Jhai ji," he continued as he

walked towards the kitchen in a veiled attempt to change the topic of the conversation while Aarti readied the dining table.

"Come on everyone, dinner is ready," invited Parvati.

"What did you make Jhai ji?" asked Akash, hovering around the table.

"Take a guess," asked Parvati with a smile on her face.

"Is it *Aloo Gobi* or *Mattar Paneer*?" asked Akash, referring to his favorite dishes with his eyes glowing like a child in the candy store.

"Both, and also your favorite *chutney*," replied Parvati with a smile.

"Also your favorite dessert, *kheer*," added the children.

"Jhai ji, you shouldn't work so hard," complained Akash.

"Beta, you know I love to cook for the family. It makes me happy."

"Thank you Jhai ji for everything you do. We are blessed to have you with us but so spoiled at the same time," replied Akash as everyone sat at the dining table.

"Your dad could eat Aloo Gobi and Mattar Paneer every day and forever," Aarti added jokingly.

"Yes, I can, but I also eat everything else happily that Jhai ji makes," replied Akash with a smile.

"Did you finish your homework for today?" asked Akash, looking at Rohit and Shreya.

"Yes dad, I finished my homework while you were gone; there wasn't that much homework today," replied Rohit, while

Shreya nodded in agreement.

"So what did you do guys do all this time?" asked Aarti. "I bet video games and TV?"

"Maybe we need to call your teachers for more homework so you would have less time for TV and video games," Aarti chuckled.

"Mom, no!" screamed Rohit. Everyone broke into laughter.

"What would you guys do with your time if all electronics were taken away for a week? No Facebook, no texting, no TV, and no video games?" Aarti continued the conversation.

"They would go crazy," interrupted Parvati before the children could answer.

"I don't know," replied Rohit innocently. "Play with friends, I guess."

"And what if you were going to be alone on a deserted island, what would you do then?" she pushed for more creative answers from the children.

"You would never let us get stranded alone on a deserted island," replied Shreya.

"I know, but that's not the point," pressed Aarti for an answer.

"Well, we would pray to the angels for help and ask them to bring us home safely," Shreya quipped.

"Do you believe in angels?" asked Aarti with a loving smile on her face.

"Yes, I do," replied Shreya with confidence and swiftly

quoted the words of Henry Ward Beecher, "Every tomorrow has two handles. We can take hold of it with the handle of anxiety or the handle of faith."

Aarti was a little surprised with Shreya's response. She thought the children might come up with some creative ways to get off of the island; however she was happy to know that the children would not give up hope under adverse conditions. Faith is not something that can be taught in schools or at home, she thought, rather, it was a state you grew into.

Shreya's innocent yet inspiring words of faith and her belief in angels resonated with everyone at the dining table. The day that had started with pain and sorrow ended with rays of hope, happiness, and hugs.

***

Akash spent the greatest part of his night tormenting himself with the falsest notions and apprehensions of things. Fear of the unknown and paralyzing flashbacks of his father falling off the cliff continued to pierce like a needle through the blanket of hope as Akash lay in bed quietly. He knew he had to be strong for his family and overcome these uncontrollable and debilitating flashbacks that had haunted him throughout his adult life.

"Yes, I want to take hold of tomorrow with the handle of faith instead of the handle of anxiety. But how?" he wondered. He prayed and prayed for angels to descend from the heavens and help him so that he would not hurt his family with his illness any longer.

While Akash lay on one side of the bed praying for miracles, Aarti prayed from the other side as she tried to chart a viable course of action for Akash. "What if Dr. Joshi says No?" she wondered. "What is it that Dr. Johnson was hoping for from Dr. Joshi that he could not do himself? I wish I had studied Psychiatry instead of Rheumatology. I would have been able to help Akash," she thought.

The cynicism and vacillating thoughts that had engulfed their minds all night were interrupted by the melodious sounds of the *ghanti* and chanting of the devotional prayers from the temple downstairs. The hypnotizing smells of sandalwood incense and *dhoop*, and the sounds of the prayers soon charged the whole house with soothing and positive energy. Parvati was chanting the devotional prayers and the *Gayatri Mantra* in Sanskrit.

"Asato maa sad-gamaya
Tamaso maa jyotir-gamaya
Mrityor-maa-mritan gamaya
Om shaantih shaantih shaantih"

Meaning…

Oh God! Please lead us from falsehood to the truth, from the unreal to the real, from darkness to light, from death to immortality. Om! Peace, peace, peace.

"Aum Bhur Bhuva Svah
Tat Savitur Varenyam
Bhargo Devasya Dhimahi
Dhiyo Yo Naha Prachodayat"

Meaning...

On the absolute reality and its planes,
On that finest spiritual light,
We meditate, as remover of obstacles
That it may inspire and enlighten us.

"Is it 5:00 in the morning already?" screamed Aarti as she jumped out of bed.

"Must be, Jhai ji is doing *puja*," said Akash, slowly opening his eyes, pretending he was waking up from a deep sleep.

"Would you like some tea or coffee?" asked Akash.

"Let me make for you today. I am sure you can use some extra rest. What would you like?"

"Some coffee would be great, thank you." replied Akash, getting out of his bed.

Soon, the invigorating aroma of freshly ground and brewed coffee along with the scents and devotional songs from the temple created a unique medley of stimulating sounds and smells of the east and west under one roof.

It was not long before everyone gathered in the kitchen for breakfast. Everyone bowed and touched Parvati's feet in a customary Indian tradition of deference and to receive her blessings.

"May God bless you with a happy, healthy, long prosperous life," uttered Parvati softly in her characteristic eloquent tone and graceful manner as she hugged everyone. She then invited everyone to the breakfast table that she had already set up with Aarti.

The first rays of morning tiptoed through the large picture window overlooking the lake as everyone sat at the breakfast table. The way the glorious morning rays streaked through the trees and the complete stillness of the water in the lake was surreal.

"What a beautiful morning!" said Akash, pointing towards the lake, where warmer than normal temperatures had brought the geese out early in search of food even though the early morning frost still covered the grass like a blanket.

"I love those little duckies swimming in the lake," said Rohit with delight as he gulped the milk.

"I wish we didn't have to go to school," added Shreya, as everyone broke into laughter.

"How come you never want to go to school?" asked Akash.

"Cause it's so boring, and I would rather spend time at home with everyone," replied Shreya.

"Be nice," chided Aarti. "You need to set a good example for Rohit."

"Whatever," replied Shreya, as she finished her breakfast.

"It's time guys, let's go," reminded Aarti as she headed towards the garage to start the car while Rohit and Shreya followed closely behind with the school bags on their shoulders.

"Have a nice day at school," said Akash as he and Parvati waved at the children.

***

At around 10 a.m., a much awaited phone call from Dr. Johnson interrupted Parvati's soft clamor of cooking in the kitchen.

"Hello," answered Parvati politely.

"Hello Grandma, this is Dr. Johnson. May I speak with Akash?"

"Just a moment please, he has been expecting your phone call," replied Parvati softly.

"Good morning Dr. Johnson," greeted Akash from his bedroom as Aarti looked on from the chair where she was reading.

"Good morning Akash! How are you feeling?"

"I am feeling much better! Thank you for asking."

"Listen! I called and spoke with Dr. Joshi this morning," Dr. Johnson continued as Akash listened impatiently.

"What did she say?" inquired Akash.

"Well! She said she was not accepting any new patients at this time," Dr. Johnson continued.

"Did she say why?"

"Not really. She said it was due to some personal reasons, but she did not elaborate. But that is not really important. For some reason, I had expected this answer already," Dr. Johnson continued.

"So what do we do now?" asked Akash.

"Well, that's why I am calling you now. I want you and Aarti, both, to call her and request for an appointment. I am sure she will relent eventually," Dr. Johnson suggested with confidence in his voice.

"I will do that," agreed Akash reluctantly while looking towards Aarti.

"Remember what I said earlier! Be persistent! Don't give up hope and keep taking your medication."

"Ok, thank you!" nodded Akash in agreement as he put the phone down.

"She said no, right?" asked Aarti as Akash nodded.

"Don't worry!" she replied as she proceeded to make the phone call herself.

"Good morning, Dr. Joshi's office, this is Carol, how may I help you?"

"Good morning Carol, this is Dr. Kumar, how are you today?"

"I am well, thank you, and you Dr. Kumar?"

"I am doing well also, thank you for asking."

"I would like to setup an appointment for my husband, Akash."

"I am sorry, but Dr. Joshi is not accepting any new patients at this time,"

"May I speak with Dr. Joshi?" asked Aarti.

"She is with a patient right now; would you like to leave a message?"

"Yes, please. She can call or beep me at any time," replied Aarti after giving the necessary information while hiding her frustration and anger.

"Don't worry, everything will be alright," said Akash in an attempt to calm Aarti. "I know how you feel having been rejected as a doctor and a concerned wife," he empathized.

"It is not about me, Akash," replied Aarti angrily. "As physicians, we are bound in our response by a common heritage of caring for the sick and the suffering," she continued.

"I completely understand your perspective; however, doctors only have so much time in a day. Besides, she only said no to accepting new patients, maybe so that she can spend more quality time with her existing patients. Also, don't forget, she might be under immense pressure from the American Medical Board as Dr. Johnson suggested," replied Akash in an attempt to calm things down a little. "Let's wait and see what she says when she calls back," he suggested after a short pause.

"Ok fine," agreed Aarti reluctantly as she turned the

music on before settling back in her chair.

What a peculiar paradox it is, wondered Akash as he pondered on the famous Tibetan saying, "When things are urgent, go slower."

"Go slower? Really?"

"Is patience really a virtue?" He wondered, looking across the room at Aarti's stern face. "People in pain have certain urgency. No surprise. Patience has always been Aarti's strength. Aarti raised two children, became a doctor, and was also an avid gardener. Her whole life has been a test of patience and endurance just like gardening -- playing in dirt, sowing seeds, trimming, clipping, pulling weeds, and harvesting a little bit every day. Then what made her so impatient today? I guess, the heart has its reasons which reason knows not of," he concluded while looking at Aarti's loving and caring face.

"I am going to help Jhai ji in the kitchen," said Aarti, putting her book away.

"Do you need my help?"

"No, thank you, get some rest instead, I will see you downstairs for lunch in a few," she replied as she headed downstairs towards the kitchen.

"Sounds great," replied Akash as he headed towards the bed for a quick nap.

It wasn't long before Akash's fitful nap was interrupted by Jhai ji's soft voice inviting him downstairs for lunch.

"I will be right there," replied Akash, slowly getting out of his bed.

"Wish the children were here also for lunch," said Aarti as she proceeded to set up the table for lunch.

"I know, the house feels so empty and lonely without the children," said Parvati.

"So, what did Dr. Johnson say this morning?" inquired Parvati, sitting at the dining table.

"Oh, he was inquiring about my health and apprising me of his conversation with Dr. Kiran Joshi," replied Akash.

"Who is Dr. Joshi?" asked Parvati, with a blank look on her face.

"Dr. Joshi is a psychiatrist that Dr. Johnson would like us to meet for a second opinion. He thought she might have some valuable insights into my recent anxiety attack," replied Akash while savoring freshly made *Choley* and *Chapati*.

"How come you did not share this with us last night?" asked Parvati.

"Well, I did not think it was a big deal. Besides, I did not want it to be our dinner conversation. I wanted to enjoy our dinner with the children."

"So, when do you see her?" inquired Parvati.

"We don't know yet, we are still working on it."

"Don't worry, everything will be alright." replied Parvati. "Everything happens for a reason," she said as she got up to clear the table with Aarti.

"How come she is always so positive, so calm, so collected despite everything life has dealt her? How does she find happiness and meaning in everything? She makes it all so easy and so peaceful. What is her secret? Does everything really happen for a reason? If so, what is the reason? What is the message? Help me get that message. Sometimes I so wish that all messages came properly labeled in life so that our faith won't be shattered," pondered Akash, sitting alone in the family room after lunch.

"Are you alright?" asked Aarti, interrupting his train of thought.

"Oh yes, I am fine," replied Akash as he tried to sit up straight.

"What were you thinking?"

"Not much, just some strange thoughts."

"Is there anything you want to talk about?"

"No, it's alright, nothing important really."

"Hey, what do you say that we all go out for dinner tonight?" asked Akash, hoping to make the best out of the situation.

"I would love to go, but I think I am going to wait for Dr. Joshi's phone call."

"Come on, it's not like you didn't give her your cell phone number," reminded Akash.

"I know, but I would rather wait to talk to her first."

"What if she doesn't call today? You would have wasted all day."

"It's not a waste, Akash. This is an important matter for me," reminded Aarti, as her face turned serious.

Miraculously, as if taking a heavenly cue, the doorbell chimed in-between their intense conversation in a divine intervention.

"The children are here," said Parvati, exulting joy as she headed quickly towards the door.

"Hi Grandma!" screamed the children with rapture as they bolted inside the house, full of vigor. They greeted Akash and Aarti with hugs and kisses.

Soon, the somber mood that had pervaded the whole house during lunch turned into one of joy as the children shared stories of their day at school, laughed, and played.

"Did you get a lot of homework today?" asked Aarti.

"Not too much," replied the children.

"Do you need help with your homework?"

"Yes, I think I'll need some help with my science homework," replied Shreya.

"And me with math," replied Rohit.

"I can help you with your science homework, and maybe your Dad can help you with your math homework," suggested Aarti.

"And I will get some snacks and milk ready for the children," said Parvati walking towards the kitchen.

"Thank you Grandma," replied the children as they settled on the table with their books and homework.

***

Grappling with dueling realities – helping children with their homework as a mother, and Akash with his illness as a wife and a doctor, Aarti did her best to focus on the present. With one eye on her cell phone waiting for Dr. Joshi's phone call, Aarti began assisting Shreya with her science homework while Akash worked with Rohit to complete his math homework.

Suddenly, Aarti leapt to her feet, startled as the phone rang.

"Hello, this is Dr. Kumar," she answered abruptly.

"Hello Dr. Kumar, this is Carol from Dr. Joshi's office."

"Oh, hello Carol, thanks for calling, I have been waiting for Dr. Joshi's phone call all day."

"I am so sorry, but Dr. Joshi has been busy all day with the patients. She asked me to give you a call and let you know that she had already spoken to Dr. Johnson about Akash and that she was not accepting any new patients at this time," replied Carol in a sincere and apologetic voice. "However, she can call you later this evening after 8:00 p.m. if you still want to talk to her," she continued politely.

An eerie silence engulfed the room as Aarti paused and contemplated for a minute before answering.

"What time does your office close?"

"We close at 5:00 p.m.; however, Dr. Joshi usually stays in her office for a few hours to catch up on her work after seeing all her patients," replied Carol.

"What time is it now?" asked Aarti.

"It's 4:45 p.m. already."

"O.K., thank you," replied Aarti.

"What happened?" asked Akash worriedly.

"Nothing," replied Aarti, as she quickly grabbed her purse.

"Where are you going?" asked Akash.

"Dr. Joshi's office," replied Aarti, heading towards the door in a hurry.

"Can I come with you?"

"No," replied Aarti. "Please take care of the kids and don't wait for me for dinner."

"Mom," screamed the children. "What's the matter?"

"I'll tell you when I come back; get your homework done," replied Aarti, pulling her car out of the garage.

"Perhaps I should follow her to Dr. Joshi's office," said Akash worriedly.

"Don't worry, she will be alright," suggested Parvati.

"But she seemed so tense and even left her cell phone in her hurry."

"She is used to working under pressure at the hospital. Besides, I think she was more determined than tensed," replied Parvati.

"Do your part, Akash. Help the children with their homework, and let her do her own part. Everything will be alright." suggested Parvati in a calm voice.

"But Jhai ji," tried to explain Akash in vain.

"Have faith," interrupted Parvati as she walked towards the kitchen to prepare dinner for the family.

***

Dr. Joshi's office was already closed for the evening by the time Aarti arrived as if the earlier encounters were not disappointing enough during the day.

"Should I knock at the door?" pondered Aarti for a few seconds before deciding against it. "I will wait outside; I don't want to disturb Dr. Joshi."

Sitting alone on a bench outside in the hallway, Aarti fixed her gaze at the front office door. An uncomfortable and eerie stillness was haunting as all offices in the building were already closed. Minutes ticked by very slowly as Aarti waited, waited and waited – 30 then 45, then more than 60 minutes, but Dr. Joshi never came out of her office. Aarti began to wonder if Dr. Joshi was actually working inside her office.

"She must still be inside. Carol said she always stayed for a few hours to catch up on her work. I will wait," decided Aarti with her eyes fixated at the front door. "A few hours of waiting outside are nothing compared to the nine months of pregnancy that I endured twice," thought Aarti.

Things which matter most must never be at the mercy of things which matter least. That is the power of positive affirmation. Patience is power. Patience is not an absence of action; rather, it is timing. It waits on the right time to act; for the right principles and in the right way.

Looking tired, Dr. Joshi finally emerged through the front doors with bleary eyes at around 9:00 p.m. after a long arduous day in her office.

"Dr. Joshi?" called Aarti, rising from the bench as her body sprang to life.

Astonished, Dr. Joshi turned towards Aarti and replied, "Yes, how can I help you?"

"Hello, I am Aarti, Akash's wife," introduced Aarti as she walked towards Dr. Joshi.

"Oh yes! Dr. Kumar, right?"

"Yes, but please call me Aarti."

"And you may call me Kiran."

"How did you know I was still here?" asked Dr. Joshi

with a surprised look on her face.

"Carol mentioned that you usually stayed in the office for a few hours after close to catch up on your work."

"How long have you been waiting outside the office?"

"Almost four hours."

"Four hours?"

"Yes, four hours," replied Aarti, as if it were not a big deal.

"I am so sorry. Why didn't you knock at the door? I would have let you in."

"I am sure you would've, but I did not want to disturb you," replied Aarti.

"What can I do for you?" asked Dr. Joshi.

"I know you are very busy, but I have come to personally request you to PLEASE accept Akash as your patient," urged Aarti.

"Please don't be upset, but as I have already mentioned to you and Dr. Johnson, I am not accepting any new patients at this time."

"I know, but this is really important to me. I love my husband, and I want him to be able to live a normal life," Aarti persisted.

"I completely understand and respect your feelings; however, there are almost three hundred equally qualified psychiatrists available in this vicinity, then why me?" asked Dr. Joshi.

"I am not sure either. However, I completely trust Dr.

Johnson and I am acting on his advice to seek your help," begged Aarti as her eyes welled up.

"Please come inside, I want to share something very personal with you so that you understand my position," replied Dr. Joshi as she opened the main entrance to her office suite.

"Please have a seat," requested Dr. Joshi.

"This is my younger brother, Varun," said Dr. Joshi, pointing towards the picture on her desk. "He has been suffering from Schizophrenia since he was twelve years old," continued Dr. Joshi.

"I am so sorry to hear that," interrupted Aarti in an attempt to console Dr. Joshi.

"My family lives in a small village with meager means. There are no hospitals for the mentally ill or even psychiatrists in the area for miles and miles. The few mental hospitals that are there are anything but mental hospitals. They are dumping grounds for families to abandon their mentally ill member, for either economic reasons or a lack of understanding and awareness of mental illness. The living conditions in many of these settings are deplorable and violate an individual's right to be treated humanely and live a life of dignity. Despite all advances in treatment, the mentally ill in these hospitals are forced to live a life of incarceration," continued Dr. Joshi with deep pain in her voice.

"There are more Indian psychiatrists abroad than in India. There are only about 4,000 psychiatrists in India to treat mentally ill patients. That is about one psychiatrist for every 300,000 Indians compared to 276 psychiatrists in the Ann Arbor area alone, serving a population of mere 114,000. That is one psychiatrist for every 412 citizens."

"Beyond the issue of stigma, the poor often don't have access to doctors. In more well-heeled enclaves, psychiatric treatment isn't covered by insurance."

"I am not even sure my parents would have been able to afford the care even if there was one available."

"I grew up watching my brother locked in a room, screaming, yelling, kicking, and hallucinating while my parents lived with the stigma and shame that came with having a mentally ill son," continued Dr. Joshi with tears in her eyes.

Feeling the deep pain of Dr. Joshi's personal story, Aarti listened with her eyes transfixed at Dr. Joshi.

"Therefore, saving my little brother became my passion and my purpose. I came to America to study psychiatry and now that I have completed my goal, I plan to go back to India, six months from now after closing down my practice," announced Dr. Joshi.

"I know I cannot save the world, but I know I can save my little brother. Now, you tell me what you would do if you were in my shoes," asked Dr. Joshi.

"I would do exactly what you are doing, Kiran," replied Aarti with a somber expression. "We are both bound by the same common purpose, to help save our loved ones."

"What if it was your husband suffering from the same illness instead of your brother?"

"What would you do?" asked Aarti.

"What would you do?"

****

04 LASTING TIES OF LOVE

It seems as if your journey never ends. Life has a way of changing things in incredible ways.

The greatest battles of life are fought out daily in the silent chambers of the soul. It's futile to fight our battles on the wrong battlefields. Gandhi once observed that "a person cannot do right in one department of life whilst attempting to do wrong in another department. Life is one indivisible whole." If we are dishonest in any role, it affects every role in our lives.

Aarti's plea for help and cogent arguments continued to haunt Kiran like a returning ghost, as she left her office. Though her eyes were fixated on the road, her mind wandered restlessly like a willow in a windstorm. She struggled to find the right balance between her oath, to serve humanity, and an urgent need to serve her brother back home as she weaved through downtown Ann Arbor.

"We are both bound by the same common purpose, to help save our loved ones. What if it was your husband suffering from the same illness instead of your brother? What would you do? What would you do?" Those words of Aarti pierced through her heart like a dagger.

"You can't stop me, I will win, I will prevail, I will not

fail," screamed Varun at the top of his voice as he tried to break the door open, and then he ran towards the window to escape from the locked room. Screaming images of her brother Varun consumed Kiran's mind.

"But humanity is our patient. We are bound in our response by a common heritage of caring for the sick and suffering," she recalled the words written in the preamble of the "Declaration of Professional Responsibility, Medicine's Social Contract with Humanity."

"But that's an illusion, not a reality," she said to herself. "I would love to help everyone in this world, but I only have so much time and energy in a day before I drop dead. It may be a simple answer but it is an obvious answer. Besides, I love my brother and I made a commitment to myself that I would return to treat him. How can I break that commitment?"

Flashing lights and wailing sirens of a police car followed Kiran as she drove along the winding Huron River Drive, overwhelmed by vacillating thoughts.

"Oh no, this is the last thing I need," sighed Kiran, pulling her car over to the shoulder.

"License and registration please," asked the policeman, as he leaned over, and looked around inside the car with his flashlight.

Kiran obediently handed her license and registration, looking worried and shaken.

"Do you know why I stopped you ma'am?" asked the cop.

"I am not sure; I know I don't speed," replied Kiran.

"You just ran a stop sign and a traffic light, ma'am," informed the cop.

"I am very sorry, I did not realize I had done that," she replied in a sincere tone, appearing exhausted with dark circles under her eyes.

"Are you a doctor?" he asked, looking at the white coat and name tag that Kiran was still wearing.

"Yes, I am."

"Is everything alright ma'am?" he inquired with concern in his voice, as he verified the documents.

"Yes, everything is fine, just a little tired, I had a long day at the office."

"Would you like me to call a cab or escort you safely to your house?" he asked in a professional manner. "Your safety, and safety of others, is of paramount concern to us."

"No, thank you. I will be fine. I don't have far to go. I really appreciate your concerns. I will be very careful. I promise."

"Please drive safely for the sake of your patients, your loved ones, and for the safety of others," he said, perhaps to lighten the weight of a hefty fine, as he handed the ticket to her.

***

Aarti sat quietly on the couch alone, in the dark, contemplating the day's events. Sensing seriousness on her face, Akash did not prod Aarti for more information and went to his room quietly. Aarti felt so moved by Kiran's personal story of love, dedication, and affection for her brother that she forgot her own personal agony, if only for a moment. Her own paradigm had shifted and she had developed respect for Dr. Joshi. She was contemplating calling Dr. Joshi in the morning to tell her not to worry about Akash and stay focused on her plans, and to wish her well in her personal journey. Aarti felt confident that she would be able to work with Dr. Johnson or any other recommendations he might have. Three-fourths of the miseries and misunderstandings in the world will disappear if we step into the shoes of our adversaries and understand their standpoint, she thought. As we really understand the other point of view, we often find our own point of view changed through increased understanding.

Aarti seemed to have found peace in her decision.

***

Kiran sat on the couch in the family room alone, in the dark, attempting to relax while soft *Hindi* music played in the background. Memories of her brother Varun engulfed her mind. The time that they spent together, playing in the fields, playing cricket, or simply playing hide and seek. Varun adored his *Didi*, as he called her, and would follow her around the house even when she was playing with her dolls.

"I will always protect you, Didi," he used to say, after getting Rakhi tied to his wrist during Raksha Bandhan celebrations as a promise, even when he was still too little to understand the meaning of the festival. Though Kiran was delighted with the Rakhi money that he gifted her, she still remembered the warmth of his hugs that were so precious and priceless.

"Raksha Bandhan is a ceremony that involves the tying of a Rakhi, a sacred thread, by a sister on her brother's wrist. This symbolizes the sister's love and prayers for her brother's well-being, and the brother's lifelong vow to protect her," taught their parents. They always made sure the proper rituals were followed for the ceremony. Kiran was to cover her head with a scarf and tie the thread of love on an empty stomach. It was a simple, yet powerful, ornament of promise, tied around the wrist as a celebration of shared trust, affection and bond. Her mother would dress her up in a green Choli, help Kiran prepare for Rakhi, teach her how to make sweets, and how to make the *Thali* of sweets look pretty. Her mother would then take out a shiny red Rakhi that had colorful beads in the center and a silver border. It sparkled brightly on Varun's wrist when the sun hit against it. He would wear that Rakhi proudly until the threads wore out.

Much has changed since then; Varun no longer understands the festival or the festivities. Kiran now ties Rakhi on Lord *Ganesha's* wrist in her temple at home in America and hopes that He will carry her wishes to Varun.

Varun was a normal, loving, and caring person as a child and at the time had no signs of mental illness. Looking back, however, perhaps there were some early warning signs. He had periods of disorganization, where it felt like his mind was falling apart: there was no center to take things in, put them together, and make sense of them. The first episode of psychosis happened when he was around 16, and he suddenly started walking home from school in the middle of the day. He began to hear voices in his mind as if he was being led towards something great. He became delusional and started hallucinating. He believed everyone around him was conspiring, talking about him, and trying to stop him from becoming great. The longer this continued, the worse it became. His behavior became volatile and aggressive. He would start fighting, yelling, and screaming when overwhelmed by voices and obstacles. "I am not going to fail," he would say. "I am too strong to fail, no matter how hard you try to throw obstacles in my way." He thought everyone was ganging up on him to build his character and to make him strong. "Adversity is the grindstone of life. Intended to polish you up, adversity also has the ability to grind you down. The impact and ultimate result depend on what you do with the difficulties that come your way," he would say of the situation. Things were not going well as they had before. No one saw things he did. No one believed the things he thought were happening to him. He saw signs and messages in things that no one else did. One day, his teacher from school handed him a card that he carried with him as a *sign* sent to him to be strong. The card read:

> *"He was born in an obscure village, the son of a peasant woman.*
>
> *He grew up in another village, where he worked in a carpenter's shop until he was thirty. Then for three years he became a wandering preacher.*

*He never wrote a book. He never held an office. He
never had a family or owned a house. He didn't go to
college. He never visited a big city. He never travelled two
hundred miles from the place where he was born. He did
none of those things one usually associates with greatness.*

He had no credentials but himself.

*He was only thirty-three when the tide of public opinion
turned against him. His friends ran away. He was
turned over to his enemies and went through a mockery
of a trial. He was executed by the state. While he was
dying, his executioners gambled for his clothing, the only
property he had on earth. When he was dead he was laid
in a borrowed grave through the pity of a friend.*

*Twenty centuries have come and gone, and today he is
the central figure of the human race and the leader of
mankind's progress. All the armies that ever marched,
all the navies that ever sailed, all the parliaments that
ever sat, all the kings that ever reigned, put together,
have not affected the life of man on this earth as much as
that* **One Solitary Life**.*"*

Everyone in the family loved Varun dearly and fought
with anyone who would call him a nut case, crazy, pagal, or
loony. Villagers would often remind the family of the
consequences of having a mentally ill brother on Kiran's future.
"No one would want to marry Kiran," they'd say. Soon the
whole family was isolated in their village but they didn't seem to
care. Varun stopped going to school, stayed in his room alone,
staring at the ceiling for the day to come when he would be
declared a winner and reach the stage of glory that he dreamed
up. Other times he would leave the house and not come back for
days, living in the streets, overcoming obstacles and adversity in
the name of building his character through sacrifices like Jesus
until another villager would inform the family of his whereabouts
or bring him home.

"I am longing to hear those words from my brother more than anything else in the world," uttered Kiran, as her eyes welled up. "Please say you will always protect me, like you used to say. You don't need to prove anything; you are already great, as my brother."

The love that Aarti and Kiran felt did not fit the traditional description of love as we know it, "A feeling, or an expression." It was more like a verb, something they both did. The unconditional sacrifices they made in the giving of self, like a mother bringing a newborn into the world.

****

05 DOCTORS OF THE SOUL

Still struggling to find the right balance between her personal and professional life, Kiran drifted off to sleep on the couch. Her sleep was fitful. Her eyebrows glistened with sweat as her body occasionally twitched as she dreamt. Her eyes were in rapid movement beneath their lids as her mind jumped and danced from image to image. In the dream, Kiran saw two armies facing each other for what appeared to be a great battle scene. Contingents of armies arrived from all parts of the country and soon the *Pandavas* led by *Arjun* had a large force of seven divisions. The *Kauravas*, led by *Duryodhan*, managed to raise an even larger army of eleven divisions. The weapons included the bows and arrows, the mace, the spear, dagger and sword. The two supreme commanders met and framed rules of ethical conduct -- dharmayuddha, for the war.

As the two armies took their positions, readied for the battle, and faced each other, Arjun, the greatest warrior, ambidextrous master archer, and commander of the Pandavas' army, was suddenly overcome by sorrow in the middle of the battle field. He stood confused and withdrawn. He saw arrayed before him, his own kinsfolk, the elders of his clan, in the opposing army, who he must kill to win.

Sensing despondency, *Lord Krishna*, who was Arjuna's

charioteer in the battle field, taught him out of extreme compassion and love, the paths of right action, right knowledge, and right devotion. He explained to Arjuna the concept of *dharma*, among other things, and made him see that it was his duty, as a warrior, to fight. He taught how to escape from this predicament, not by mere escape from the burdens of the worldly life or avoidance of responsibilities, but by remaining amidst the humdrum of life and facing them squarely with a sense of fearlessness, detachment, and stability of mind, accepting God as the Doer. He taught that salvation was not possible for those who wanted to escape from life and activity. Those who remained amidst society, unafraid of the burdens of life, and lived a life of sacrifice fully surrendering to God were in fact more qualified for it.

The epochal event, the eighteen days of war of Kurukshetra, also known as Mahabharata, along with divine guidance of Lord Krishna, known as Bhagawat Gita, or the song of Lord, continued to play out in Kiran's dream throughout the night. She startled awake at the crack of the dawn, her body full of sweat, with scenes of death and destruction everywhere still playing in her mind.

Sitting quietly at the edge of the couch, rubbing her eyes, contemplating, and organizing her thoughts, Kiran uttered, "I must accept my responsibility, my Dharma, just like Arjun -- without attachment or expectations, and leave the results in God's hands."

Feeling confident, and at peace with her decision, Kiran arrived early in her office that morning to call Aarti and Dr. Johnson before starting her busy day.

Aarti and Kiran chatted for a few minutes before Kiran informed Aarti of her decision to accept Akash as her patient. "I will call Dr. Johnson and ask for Akash's files to be sent over as soon as possible. However, I will need a couple of weeks to go over his history before I set up an appointment to meet Akash," informed Kiran.

"That would be fine," replied Aarti.

"I also want to make you aware that my medical practice is being investigated by the American Psychiatric Association for adopting 'controversial practices' as reported anonymously by someone," continued Kiran as her voice became serious.

"I was already made aware of that by Dr. Johnson, and I am not concerned at all after meeting with you last night. I feel safe and secure," confirmed Aarti, with confidence in her voice.

"In that case, I will need you and Akash to sign a letter of understanding, giving me complete freedom, as well as full support of your family in treating Akash before we proceed."

"That won't be a problem; we will stop by your office and sign the letter as soon as you have it ready."

"Also, I still plan to go back to India within six months, which means my schedule will be particularly tight, and I will need you to be flexible with available appointments," requested Kiran.

"That won't be a problem," agreed Aarti without hesitation.

"And finally, I want you to know that I will do my best to treat Akash, but please don't expect any miracles," continued Kiran.

"We will accept your help graciously and leave the rest in God's hands," replied Aarti with a choking voice, as her eyes welled up with gratitude.

"In that case, I will go ahead and call Dr. Johnson and ask him to send Akash's files over and ask Carol to set up an appointment in two weeks. That will give me enough time to review Akash's files."

Kiran wasted no time and reached Dr. Johnson

immediately after completing her conversation with Aarti. Dr. Johnson was excited to hear that Kiran had agreed to see Akash as her patient and offered unconditional professional help. He also promised to send Akash's files over immediately to facilitate treatment. Kiran, however, wanted to know Dr. Johnson's expectations and reasons behind his decision to refer Akash to her despite allegations of "controversial practices" swirling around her practice.

"It is because of it, not despite it that I referred the case over to you Dr. Joshi. We need more psychiatrists like you who are willing to color outside the lines and challenge the status quo. As you well know, the mind is highly complex and enigmatic. However, I am afraid that many psychiatrists today are overly simplifying our profession and relegating it to an ancillary position. They are simply asking patients a series of questions about their symptoms and labeling those symptoms into a category described in the DSM (Diagnostic and Statistical Manual of Mental Disorders). They think that they understand their patients, when all they are doing is assigning labels and writing prescriptions. Our goal should be to help patients become happy and fulfilled, not just to keep them functional," continued Dr. Johnson. "Another area of my concern is our lack of understanding of how the expectations and beliefs of the sufferer shape their suffering. The problem is the overall thrust that comes from being at the heart of one globalizing culture. It is as if one version of human nature is being presented as definitive, and one set of ideas about pain and suffering....There is no one definitive psychology. That's where we need psychiatrists like you with different cultural backgrounds who also have the courage to challenge those deeply flawed theories and one shoe fits all approach. I am not suggesting that we abandon our hard-won knowledge of medicine and nomothetic research, but rather to enhance it with understanding that each patient's unique experiential reality is the essence of psychiatric practice, and mental health care in general."

"I completely understand and respect your feelings, Dr. Johnson, and I will do my best to exceed your expectations," replied Kiran as they concluded their conversation.

***

Over the next two weeks, Kiran pored over the records supplied by Dr. Johnson's office with the diligence and focus of a medical student preparing for the medical board exams. She left no stone unturned, often working late at night, alone in her office, going through every single detail in Akash's file. She could not help but notice the brevity of Dr. Johnson's meetings with Akash and scantiness of his notes this year compared to previous years. She wondered if he also had stopped giving psychotherapy to his patients like many other psychiatrists -- a growing trend amongst psychiatrists.

Hoping to find answers, she paged Dr. Johnson. It wasn't long before Dr. Johnson returned her request for a phone call and confirmed that he was no longer providing psychotherapy as a rule, except when deemed absolutely necessary at the time.

"Is that because of the parsimonious reimbursement policies of health insurance companies that discourage psychotherapy by psychiatrists?" asked Dr. Joshi.

"First, it is not that I am more comfortable with molecules than with motives, but we all have to adapt to the changing needs of our patients and trends in the industry. Psychotherapy can be provided by psychologists and social workers who can charge less because they don't go to medical schools like we do. Therefore, it is no longer economically viable to continue to provide psychotherapy. Besides, there is no evidence that psychiatrists, in general, provide higher quality psychotherapy than psychologists or social workers," replied Dr. Johnson.

"True, but how many patients actually go to seek therapy from psychologists once they leave their psychiatrist? Has Akash sought help from a trained therapist since this change?" asked Dr. Joshi.

"Not yet, though I highly recommended one."

"Exactly my point," stressed Dr. Joshi.

"But ultimately, the responsibility falls on the patient's shoulders. The patient must seek proper help and care," argued Dr. Johnson. "I hope you are not trying to associate this change with his recent fall and worsening condition now, are you?" asked Dr. Johnson jokingly.

"Not at all, but I also can't rule out any possibilities as a psychiatrist," replied Dr. Joshi.

"Well! Psychotherapy and pharmacotherapy do not occupy two totally different realms of psychiatry. Psychotherapy does not operate in a vacuum apart from medication. This is a false dichotomy. I often spend more time providing supportive psychotherapy than dealing with medication issues if a patient's needs warrant it. But that was not the case with Akash. Above all, the first element in any therapy is self-disclosure. Akash has always been a highly private person and an evasive one, never fully disclosing about his pain, suffering or internal turmoil. He simply hides or plays down his suffering. Maybe it is cultural. You can't treat the root causes of something you don't know with therapy. In that case, you end up treating symptoms with medications and manage the pain. What else can you do?" exclaimed Dr. Johnson in a frustrated tone.

"Does he belong to any support groups?" asked Dr. Joshi.

"No, he does not. He did not think it was necessary when I suggested one," replied Dr. Johnson.

"Don't you think it will be even harder for Akash to open up to a female psychiatrist if he is so evasive and private about his personal life?" asked Dr. Joshi.

"It is certainly possible, but culturally, you have an advantage. You can probably discern his emotions better that I can," replied Dr. Johnson in a supportive manner.

"I understand the whole situation better now, after our conversation. I sincerely appreciate your time and support in this matter," said Dr. Joshi in a sincere tone.

"Please feel free to call me anytime if you need further help. Nothing will make me happier than to see Akash become happy and fulfilled. I know we can do it by working together," replied Dr. Johnson.

"Yes indeed. Together we will," assured Dr. Joshi as she concluded the conversation.

****

06 BOWL OF BLESSINGS

It is often in the darkest skies, we see the brightest stars.

Much relieved by Dr. Joshi's decision to accept Akash as her patient, Akash and Aarti returned to work while anxiously awaiting the first appointment. Hope dawned in the distance like a sail for the family. Everyone at the office was glad to see Akash and welcomed him back with open arms. There was a great sense of camaraderie among the professors and staff in his department. True to its motto of "building great places to work," the university took great pride and went out of its way to build a culture of goodwill and rapport. Flowers and cards from students, professors, staff, and other well-wishers adorned Akash's office. The dean, among others, welcomed Akash back and reminded him to take it easy for a while, go slowly, look after himself, and let the body recover. These were the same words uttered just a couple of months earlier after another anxiety attack, but Akash had no time or patience for convalescing. He always worked diligently and took much pride in his work and did not want to be seen as a sickly or a weak person. Above all, he loved his work and taught his students with passion and purpose like a gospel. During stressful times, he would often take inspiration from the words of J. Reuben Clark Jr. that adorned the wall of his office:

"As teachers you stand upon the highest peak in education, in priceless value in far-reaching effect with that which deals with man as he was in the eternity of yesterday, as he is in the mortality of today, and as he will be in the forever of tomorrow. Not only time but eternity is your field."

Equally excited was Aarti and her staff to resume daily operations of her medical practice that had been put on hold. Aarti ran her practice just like her family at home: congenial, yet professional. Her patients, mostly older, loved the way they were treated with love, affection, respect, and dignity. It was like a family reunion.

***

"Your Journey Begins Now!" A welcome note from Dr. Joshi greeted Akash as he returned from work.

Dear Akash,

Welcome to The New Horizons Integrated and Holistic Psychiatry. My name is Kiran Joshi, and I appreciate the confidence and trust you have placed in us and I look forward to meeting you personally and professionally.

Mental illness feels just as bad, or worse, than any other illness – only you cannot see it.

It takes courage to seek help and guidance. We honor and support this step you are taking towards deeper mental, emotional, and physical health and well-being.

Our philosophy of care governs everything we do for you. It consists of the following key elements.

We believe that the health and balance of all the systems of the body, mind, emotions, and spirit are interconnected and that your personal health is interconnected with the community and Earth in which you live.

We believe that you are a unique person and that there are no "one-size-fits-all" approaches to enhancing your mental health. Therefore, I will develop a treatment plan with you involved that takes into consideration your uniqueness, your gifts, and all levels that make up your total health.

We will work together as a team. You will be given education, guidance, direct therapeutic interventions, and expertise to help you learn about yourself, find balance, heal, and maintain wellness. I ask that you do your part and actively participate in your healing and treatment process. It is only in this way that lasting change can truly occur.

Never be ashamed of having bad days, weeks, or even months -- because they show your inner strength, even if you can't see it yourself at the time. And you are in good company. Great leaders like Winston Churchill, Abraham Lincoln, Mahatma Gandhi, Martin Luther King Jr., and John F. Kennedy, all suffered from some kind of mental illness in their lives.

Over the next few days, you will be receiving additional notes and materials from our office. I ask that you read and complete all the necessary information before our first meeting for a meaningful and productive session.

Your journey begins now!

Sincerely,

Kiran Joshi, M.D.

***

"Interesting," said Akash with a smile on his face.

"What is it?" asked Aarti, as everyone gathered around the kitchen table.

"A welcome letter from Dr. Joshi."

"May I see it?"

"Sure."

"Very impressive, I should create something so personal and welcoming for my new patients."

"That was pretty quick! We just talked to her a few days ago about this appointment," wondered Akash.

"I know. She is closing her practice in six months to return to India," replied Aarti.

"You didn't say anything about that," said Akash.

"I did not want to add to your anxiety."

"How was your day at work?" interrupted Jhai ji as she served snacks to Aarti and Akash.

"It was good! Things are getting back to normal again," replied Aarti, while going through the children's homework.

"Guess what? I am so excited!" interrupted Shreya with a huge grin, both arms in the air, and dancing.

"What is it?" exclaimed Akash with a smile.

"She probably bought more clothes or something," replied Rohit in a grumbling voice.

"No silly! It's Thanksgiving break next week!"

"So, are you excited about Thanksgiving or the school break?" asked Aarti, with her eyebrows raised.

"Both."

"Yeah right," grumbled Rohit, as everyone broke into laughter.

"Why are you being so grumpy today?" asked Aarti, as she straightened his hair with her fingers.

"He is always grumpy," taunted Shreya.

"No, I am not," replied Rohit angrily and making faces at Shreya.

"Yuh-huh."

"Alright, alright, cut it out you two. Finish your homework," chided Aarti.

"I love Thanksgiving! It is such a wonderful family holiday, peaceful and relaxing," said Akash, interrupting a brief silence at the table.

"I agree. Everyone gets in a wonderful holiday spirit because of Thanksgiving and Christmas," added Aarti.

"I want lots of presents for Christmas," said Shreya with joy and excitement in her voice.

"Me too," added Rohit, briefly stopping his homework.

Conversation and activities continued through the evening, followed by dinner before everyone said good night and left for their rooms.

A much anticipated call from Dr. Joshi's office followed within two days after the letter. Luckily, the appointment was on

Wednesday, the day before Thanksgiving, therefore it required no last minute changes to his teaching schedule because of the holidays.

***

Deja Vu All Over Again

Dr. Joshi's office was located in an upper class neighborhood on the outskirts of town. Carol greeted Akash with great enthusiasm at the front desk and walked him to the waiting area after collecting all the necessary forms that he had filled out and brought with him. The waiting area was quite pleasant with modern colors and comfortable furniture. Akash sat alone, quietly looking at a fairly large selection of newspapers and magazines for men, women, and children of all ages. The other corner had a large table with complimentary coffee and water bottles. For a minute, Akash sensed it might be a long wait because of all the amenities to make patients feel comfortable while they waited. It turned out not to be the case. It wasn't long before Dr. Joshi arrived to receive Akash with a gentle hand shake and a soft smile. Dressed professionally, in a grey, knee length skirt suit, white coat, and glasses, her demeanor appeared refined, confident, and responsible. Petite with long brown hair and a dark complexion, she appeared younger than her age, but every bit Indian.

"Hello, I am Dr. Joshi, please follow me." Akash followed Dr. Joshi like an obedient child in school. Her office was tastefully decorated just like the waiting room, with neutral colors and modern furniture. The room was brightly lit with the daylight coming through a large picture window. Sheer white curtains with soft rose colored drapes and decorations covered the double doors opening up to the balcony; the perfect setting for sunshine lovers. A modern painting adorned one side of the wall while an impressive array of degrees from Yale and other universities validated her competency in the field of psychiatry. Various healthy plants created a home like atmosphere, instead of tall book cases filled with boring medical texts and literature. Akash hated seeing those books in doctors' offices as if they had all the answers in the world about your problems. "Many doctors are simply unaware of the impact of their setting on their patients' psyches," thought Akash. He felt welcomed, at ease, comfortable, and most importantly, safe. The two sat across from each other in a more informal setting than the one used by Dr. Johnson, who conversed from behind a desk.

"Before we begin, I want to assure you of complete confidentiality," said Dr. Joshi. She then discussed his recent blood test report, physical exam, and family history, all of which were normal. While medical records were easy to discuss, Akash felt extremely uncomfortable discussing his personal life details as it was no one's business. Akash loved his privacy and guarded it with full armor, rarely giving details to anyone. People at the university often called him a mysterious man. The invasive and voyeuristic nature of psychiatry was uncomfortable, to say the least, to Akash. In no other situation would it be even mildly appropriate to ask another individual about intimate personal details including his sexual relationship with spouse, sexual fantasies, and early childhood experiences. Psychiatrists possess a desire to delve deep into the depths of a forbidden zone, the same way a surgeon cuts open someone's sternum. Neither is a routine activity of daily living and both can be painful, yet necessary.

"Do you sleep well at night? asked Dr. Joshi.

"Yes, for the most part."

"What worries you when you can't sleep well?"

"We all worry at times, nothing serious really."

"Can you be more specific, please?"

"Like I said; nothing really serious."

"Do you feel guilty, ashamed, or regretful of any events in life that bother you and keep you awake at night?"

"None that I can think of," replied Akash, looking the other way.

"Any work related worries?"

"None."

"How do you get along with your wife, children, and mother?"

"Very well, I love them very much."

"How does your wife feel having your mother living at home; does she ever complain or argue about that?"

"No, she seems fine and quite understanding."

"Tell me about your father."

"He died when I was young. I was about seven years old."

"How did he die?"

"It was an accident."

"Can you tell me exactly what happened?"

"He slipped and fell to his death while we were on a hiking trip," replied Akash, as he rubbed his forehead and his jaws tightened. "And I am sure you were provided with a police report in my file."

"Yes, I was; however, I want to hear from you."

"Well, I just told you."

"Do you miss your father?"

"Who wouldn't?"

"I am only interested about you."

"Yes, I do!"

"And your mother never remarried, being that she became a widow at such a young age?"

"No, she did not. She is very traditional in that sense."

"Does she ever discuss your father at home?"

"No, she does not."

"What are you most proud of in life," asked Dr. Joshi in an attempt to give Akash some breathing room, sensing his discomfort and irritation with more intimate invasive questions related to his childhood memories about his father.

"My family, my job, and my book that I am writing," replied Akash with a sigh of relief.

"What is the book about?"

"The Golden Triangle: How India, Pakistan and Bangladesh, three impoverished countries, can achieve greatness and reduce poverty through trade and leveraging synergies."

"Sounds interesting, but haven't others before you made a similar argument?

"I am sure they have; does that make my argument any less important?" argued Akash.

"No, but is it even feasible, given deeply rooted animosities among these three countries?"

"Do you have all the answers for every mental illness?" asked Akash.

"Not at all, but we are always learning and striving."

"Exactly my point; besides, my book focuses more on the strong common heritage we all share, new opportunities created by technology and other new developments," replied Akash as he cited a quote by Marion Zimmer Bradley.

> *"It has never been, and never will be easy work! But the road that is built in hope is more pleasant to the traveler than the road built in despair, even though they both lead to the same destination."*

"That sounds wonderful," replied Dr. Joshi in a sincere tone of voice, as she bowed her head. "Is there anything I can do to help?"

"None that I can think of right now; thank you though for your kind gesture."

"Do you celebrate Thanksgiving?" asked Dr. Joshi.

"Yes, we do."

Dr. Joshi then picked up a gift that was lying on a side table and handed it to Akash.

"What is it?" asked Akash with curiosity.

"It's a bowl of blessings," replied Dr. Joshi with a smile on her face.

"A bowl of blessings?" asked Akash with a puzzled look on his face.

"You see, too often in life, people let their problems, difficulties, and tragedies overshadow everything that is good in their daily lives," said Dr. Joshi.

"I would like you to fill this bowl with as many blessings as you can count sincerely, and then read them out loud to your family at Thanksgiving dinner. Cultivating an 'attitude of gratitude' has been linked to better health, sounder sleep, less anxiety and depression, higher long term satisfaction with life, and kinder behavior toward others, including romantic partners," continued Dr. Josh after a short pause.

"Have a happy Thanksgiving and please feel free to call me if you have any questions or if you just want to talk about something."

"I will do that, and happy Thanksgiving to you and your loved ones also," reciprocated Akash, as they shook hands and concluded their meeting.

****

07 BEHIND THE CALM FACADE

It was crisp, clear, and cold under the blue sky. Dressed casually in sweat pants, a hooded sweatshirt, and sneakers, Dr. Joshi greeted Akash with a smile and firm handshake. Akash was perplexed and surprised at the venue selected for his appointment: Gallup Park, located along Huron River and Geddes pond with scenic walkways that traverse small islands with bucolic pedestrian bridges. They walked towards the Furstenberg Nature Area within the park. Colorful Christmas lights and decorations added extra charm to the park's serene landscape.

Dr. Joshi often conducted her sessions outdoors, out of her power base and into parks and hills. She believed it was much more of an equal turf and provided more parity rather than sitting face-to-face in the office. This was especially true with men, she believed. Men have difficulty with eye contact in the office, chair-to- chair, knee-to-knee, revealing very private and possibly painful things. Walking side-by-side can help a man become vulnerable. Sitting is a passive, deflated posture. Walking is literally moving ahead. People feel like they are moving forward in their issues. They can tackle things better and faster.

"So! How was your Thanksgiving?" asked Dr. Joshi, as they walked, trailing behind vapors from their mouths and noses.

"It was great! How was yours?" asked Akash with politeness while hiding his curiosity by rubbing his hands to stay warm.

"It was good... peaceful and relaxing, but I miss the family dinners back home. It gets a bit lonely sometimes," explained Dr. Joshi.

"I didn't realize you lived alone, or I would have invited you over."

"Thank you very much! That is very nice of you to say that."

"So, tell me exactly what happened on that Diwali night." she said, as the two walked forward without making an eye contact.

"Does that happen often?"

"Not often and not as severely."

"What other symptoms do you feel besides dizziness and light headedness when that happens?"

"Heart palpitations, sweating, shakiness, shortness of breath, and a choking feeling, as if I was being smothered."

"Do you experience nightmares?"

"Yes, sometimes."

"What triggers such a strong response?"

"I don't know," replied Akash as he became tense and started rubbing his neck and temples.

"Are you sure you don't know, or you can't put it in words?" prodded Dr. Joshi.

"I don't know; sometimes it seems like I can't control what is happening to me. I wish I had all the answers. Sometimes I think I worry too much and internalize everything that happens to me," replied Akash as he became immersed in his thoughts.

"All these years, all that money," thought Akash. It began when he was seven or eight years old, an anxiety ridden child who did not want to go to school in the morning and had difficulty falling asleep at night. One psychiatrist after another had wanted him to illuminate his puzzling behavior and onerous symptoms. His dissatisfaction with the whole process made him wonder and contemplate if it was time for a change – whether at long last, it might be time to strike out on his own, and weather his internal and external vicissitudes alone, perilous as that prospect might appear to a person who hadn't been without a psychiatrist's support in recent memory. He thought of various therapists and their different styles of treatment, most of them Freudian-derived to a greater or lesser extent, all of which had turned him off in one way or another. In therapy that was more psychoanalytically oriented, he tended to get himself trapped in long-ago traumas, identifying himself as a terrified boy. This imaginative position would eventually destabilize him, kicking off feelings of rage and despair that would become a spiral down into a debilitating depression, in which he could not seem to retrieve the pieces of his present life. He didn't know whether this was because of the therapist's lack of skill, some essential flaw in the psychoanalytical method, or some irreparable injury done to him long ago. The last time he engaged in this style of therapy for an extended period of time with an analyst who kept coaxing him to dredge up more and more painful, ever earlier memories, he ended up in a hospital. When he got out, he sought out a different psychiatrist who would take a more contained, present-oriented approach, with far less time and energy spent trying to excavate distant hurts and regrets. Someone who may have the convictions of a Freudian, but he would also have the manner of a strategic advisor, cheering him on in his daily life. And yet, after seeing the new psychiatrist for several months, he felt that he was doing himself an injustice by merely skimming the surface, leaving himself vulnerable to the kind of massive subterranean conflict. He feared it would sooner or later come out of nowhere and hit him hard once again.

Would he ever, he wondered, manage to find the right

mix? The style of therapy that would fit his particular mold? Did that even exist?

Akash knew he wasn't the most promising candidate – he was, in fact, a prime example of what was referred to within the profession as a *difficult* patient, with his clamorous, evasive ways, disregard for boundaries, and serial treatments. But he thought, someday he would get lucky enough to find that right therapist, a practitioner, who would not only understand his lifelong sorrow and anger in an empathetic fashion, but also be able to relieve him of them. Just as some people believe in the idea of soul mates, he held fast to the conviction that his perfect therapeutic match was out there. If only he looked hard enough, he would find that person, and then the demons that haunted him would become, easier to manage.

Therapy, as Freud himself made clear, was never about finding a cure for what ailed you. Its aim was always more modest. Freud described it as an effort to convert *hysterical misery* into *common unhappiness*, which suggested a rather minimalist framework against which to judge progress. There was no absolute goal, no lifetime guarantee; no telling how much therapy was enough therapy, no foolproof way of knowing when you've gotten everything out of it that you wanted.

Patients want answers, whereas psychoanalysts ask questions. Patients want advice, but psychoanalysts are trained not to give advice. Patients want support and love. Psychoanalysts offer interpretations and insight. Patients want to feel better; analysts talk about character change.

Even to this day, Akash wasn't sure if he knew anyone whose character had been genuinely transformed because of therapy. If anything, most people seemed to emerge as more backed-up versions of themselves. Akash was a firm believer in the philosophy that people do not change that much. He always shared a famous fable to make this point with his students.

> *Once upon a time there was a scorpion asking a frog to carry him across a river. The frog is afraid of being stung during the trip, but the scorpion argues that if it stung*

the frog, the frog would sink and the scorpion would drown. The frog agrees and begins carrying the scorpion, but midway across the river the scorpion does indeed sting the frog, dooming them both. When asked why, the scorpion points out that this is its nature.

"What are you thinking?" asked Dr. Joshi, tapping on his shoulder as if she read his mind.

"Oh, nothing really," replied Akash, hiding his thoughts.

"Your urine test came back and it shows a low secretion of cortisol and high secretion of catecholamine with a norepinephrine/cortisol ratio consequently higher. This is in contrast to the fight-or-flight response, in which both catecholamine and cortisol levels are elevated after exposure to a stressor. Your brain catecholamine levels are high and corticotrophin-releasing factor (CRF) concentrations are high. Together, these results suggest abnormality in the hypothalamic-pituitary-adrenal (HPA) axis."

"What does it all mean?" asked Akash with a puzzled look on his face.

"Well, simply put, because cortisol is normally important in restoring homeostasis after stress response, it is thought that trauma survivors with low cortisol experience a poorly contained – that is, longer and more distressing – response, setting the stage for PTSD (Post-Traumatic Stress Disorder). PTSD is a mental health condition that's triggered by a terrifying event. While usually associated with combat, PTSD has been linked to many psychologically traumatic events. It generates severe anxiety along with flashbacks, nightmares, and anger as well as uncontrollable thoughts about the event. Symptoms typically start within three months of a traumatic event. In a small number of cases, though, PTSD symptoms may not appear until years after the event," continued Dr. Joshi, briefly stopping for a passing row of ducks. "Unlike physical wounds, PTSD is invisible, intangible. I want to stress the point however, that this is not my diagnosis; at least not yet."

"So what's next?" asked Akash with a grim look on his face as the two continued their walk.

"I have scheduled a Magnetoencephalography test (or MEG for short) for you for next week. It is a relatively new, non-invasive brain imaging technology recently developed and is going to become an increasingly important player in mankind's quest to understand human brain functions, psychology, and neuroscience."

"How is it different from CT scans (Computed Tomography) or an MRI (Magnetic Resonance Imaging)?" asked Akash.

"The MEG machine itself resembles a giant, space-age salon hair dryer with 248 sensors that pick up miniscule magnetic signals that result when brain cells talk to each other through electrical impulses. Whereas CT scans and MRIs record brain signals every few seconds, MEGs can do it by the millisecond, catching biomarkers and brain activity that the other tests inevitably miss. MEG machines are fast, sensitive and provide an accurate way to measure electrical activity in the brain. MEG records brain activity essentially in real time—down to a thousandth of a second. That's how fast brain cells talk with each other. Other types of scans involve lags of three seconds or longer. In trying to understand brain function that time difference is critical. It's not actually a type of brain scan that uses radiation or magnetic fields; it is a technology that takes a reading of brain activity. You can think about it as a very sophisticated EEG (electroencephalogram) where electrical leads are placed on the scalp. The room is shielded from the earth's magnetism so that the sensors in the scanner can read the activity from the surface of your brain."

"How long and how difficult is the reading process?"

"The scanning session is one minute, with readings taken a thousand times per second. People find it easy and the most we ask them to do in this study is close their eyes for a time and open their eyes for a time and focus on a spot. It is very safe, has no risks, and is easy, unless you have problems lying still for a few minutes."

"What are you seeing in the activity of patients with PTSD?"

"By analyzing the interconnections among parts of the brain's surface, we see patterns of miscommunication that define a PTSD stamp."

"What did the results show from your study?"

"That we are able to accurately classify people with PTSD 95 – 100 percent of the time. That there is a brain pattern or "stamp" that is so distinctive that it allows us to identify PTSD."

"What's next after this test?"

"I will need you to be more forthcoming about your past, especially all traumatic experiences that you have encountered, more specifically, about your father and the conditions under which he died in detail. I know this can be very difficult but it is necessary for me to know. I will also need to talk to your mother, your children, and your wife before I know for sure what I will need to do next."

"What does my family have to do with all this?" asked Akash with an uncomfortable look on his face.

"As I said, I need to know everything if I am to treat you."

"But you already have all the details."

"I don't mean simply the police report or other scanty information that was provided to Dr. Johnson."

"What good is this MEG test then, if I still have to dredge up the traumatic events that generate PTSD?" asked Akash with obvious irritation on his face.

"Well, PTSD is largely a subjective process involving mental-health workers conducting structured interviews with patients suffering PTSD-like symptoms. The MEG test can prove that one has PTSD. It gives a name to one's illness in an objective manner. But the treatment will still depend on one's suffering."

"You don't sound convinced, do you?" asked Dr. Joshi as she tried to make eye contact with Akash.

"Not really," replied Akash bluntly.

"I am sure you would agree that the mind is highly complex and enigmatic. Many wonder how we can study such an intricate, seemingly abstract and extremely sophisticated thing. Even if you look inside the brain, as in an autopsy or during surgery, all you see is gray matter. Thoughts, cognition, emotions, memories, dreams, and perceptions, cannot be seen physically, like a skin rash or heart defect. We are unable to observe the mind directly; however, virtually all our actions, feelings, and thoughts are influenced by the functioning of our minds. To make matters even more complicated, people suffer differently. Culture plays a huge role. Mental illnesses are not discrete entities like the polio virus. Mental illnesses have never been the same either in prevalence or in form but are inevitably sparked and shaped by the ethos of particular times and places. Expectations and beliefs of the sufferer shape their suffering," argued Dr. Joshi with confidence. "The Indian society," she argued, "has traditionally been underpinned by values which emphasize diligence, stoicism, modesty, and self-sacrifices. Individual concerns are secondary. Preserving dignity, or face, especially for the family, is paramount. Indians, for instance, hold that the ability not to talk about distressing experiences is a sign of maturity. This runs counter to the typical assumption of trauma counselors in the west, that a healing catharsis can be achieved through truth telling."

"Now you tell me, what you will do under such circumstances?" asked Dr. Joshi looking at Akash's face for answers.

"But you don't understand, you weren't there," replied Akash with clear signs of grief as his muscles tightened, eyes closed, and fists clinched."

"What is it that I don't understand, Akash?"

"No, you can't understand because you weren't there," repeated Akash over and over as his eyes welled up.

***

Akash and Dr. Joshi walked quietly to their cars, totally unprepared for the winter chill that had descended unexpectedly upon them.

****

08 BURDENS OF THE SOUL

A few weeks later…

It was a snowy Friday afternoon in January, and Akash was inching along State Street during rush hour with his family. His mood was as gray as the sky on his way to Dr. Joshi's office. Many questions raced through his mind as he ruminated over his decision to authorize Dr. Joshi for this predicament. He did not want his family to worry over his personal problems, let alone participate in any type of questioning or counseling in a psychiatrist's office, even worse, in his presence. He had protected his privacy with full armor, and his family from unnecessary grief. Intuitively, in his bones, Akash felt the calm that usually preceded a storm. He felt a loss of control over this situation which made him uncomfortable, to say the least. He prayed and wished the traffic would come to a standstill so that they would miss their appointment. Unfortunately, his wishes did not come true. Maybe God had different plans.

Carol greeted the Kumar family with a sincere warm smile, and seated them in the waiting room. The office area was quiet as most of the staff had already left for the day. It was almost closing time. An eerie calm prevailed in the waiting area as Akash, Aarti, Shreya, and Rohit sat quietly waiting for Dr.

Kiran Joshi to arrive. A large plaque, reading "Code of Ethics," among other things, adorned the walls that read:

Declaration of Professional Responsibility
Medicine's Social Contract with Humanity

Declaration

We, the members of the world community of physicians, solemnly commit ourselves to:

I. Respect human life and the dignity of every individual.

II. Refrain from supporting or committing crimes against humanity and condemn all such acts.

III. Treat the sick and injured with competence and compassion and without prejudice.

IV. Apply our knowledge and skills when needed, though doing so may put us at risk.

V. Protect the privacy and confidentiality of those for whom we care and breach that confidence only when keeping it would seriously threaten their health and safety or that of others.

VI. Work freely with colleagues to discover, develop, and promote advances in medicine and public health that ameliorate suffering and contribute to human well-being.

VII. Educate the public about present and future threats to the health of humanity.

VIII. Advocate for social, economic, educational, and political changes that ameliorate suffering and contribute to human well-being.

IX. Teach and mentor those who follow us for they are the future of our caring profession.

Akash questioned in his mind how this meeting was in line with "respecting the dignity of every individual?"

Minutes of waiting felt like an eternity as the clock ticked ever so slowly, while Akash continued to pray for miracles to calm his anxious mind.

"Good afternoon, everyone," greeted Dr. Joshi with a smile, as everyone stood up in deference and shook her hand one by one. Dr. Joshi did not appear to be in any hurry as she spent the next several minutes talking to Shreya and Rohit until Carol briefly interrupted their conversation to say that she was leaving for the day. Everyone followed Dr. Joshi soon thereafter to her office where she reminded Akash why this family meeting was necessary.

Akash nodded in reluctance with a grim look on his face.

"I want you also to know that I had the privilege and pleasure of meeting and talking to all of your family members individually over the past few weeks. You have a wonderful family and you should be very proud of them. They all love you very much. I had asked them not to discuss the details of our meeting with you, at least not for now," continued Dr. Joshi while Akash sat quietly in disbelief.

"I hope you will forgive me but I need to ask you a few very personal questions. Please be honest," said Dr. Joshi as her face turned serious. "What are you hiding from your family? What is on your mind? What is bothering you that you don't care to share?"

"Are you having an affair?"

"What!" Akash screamed in disbelief.

"Are you having an affair?" repeated Dr. Joshi with her

hands folded and a serious look on her face.

"Are you crazy?" screamed Akash in disbelief as he stood erect. "How dare you ask me such a stupid question?"

"It is not a stupid question Mr. Kumar, please answer."

"Let's go," ordered Akash in an authoritative voice to his family. "We don't have to put up with this nonsense," as he walked towards the door fuming with anger and disbelief. "No wonder you are closing your practice. Who would want to put up with such an irresponsible stupid doctor?"

"Come on everyone, let's go, I am done with her."

"Go right ahead, Mr. Kumar," taunted Dr. Joshi. "But remember, your demons will continue to haunt you and your anxiety attacks won't stop if you walk out that door today. There will be more of the same. More emergency room visits, and your wife staying up all night by your side. Your children and mother in pain. Is that what you want?" challenged Dr. Joshi. "Is that what you want?" she repeated with equal firmness and seriousness on her face. "Why don't you just leave them instead of putting them through this pain?"

"Akash, please answer the question, I am a grown woman. I can accept the truth, whatever that might be," joined Aarti in the conversation with her soft voice.

"What!" screamed Akash in disbelief as he turned towards Aarti while his body was shaking with anger and obvious pain in his eyes.

"Yes Dad, we will still love you no matter what," said Shreya and Rohit as they held Aarti's hand.

"No, No, No! You know I love you more than anything else in the world," cried Akash as he hugged Shreya and Rohit with tears rolling down on his face. "How can you even think of such a thing?"

"Then what is it that bothers you so much? Gives you

nightmares, flashbacks, anxiety, and pain to a point that you would collapse on the stage?" asked Dr. Joshi.

"No, you won't understand, you weren't there. You can't understand," mumbled Akash in pain with his head down on the table as he sobbed.

"What is it, Akash?" asked Aarti as she came closer to Akash and held his hand. "Is it about *Baoji?*"

"I couldn't do anything to save him. He kept screaming for help but I could not do anything to save him; he died there and I could not do anything to save him," sobbed Akash uncontrollably in Aarti's lap as Shreya and Rohit rested their heads on his shoulders and cried.

There were enough tears in the room to fill an ocean. No one had ever seen Akash in such a vulnerable and painful state before. He appeared, at least on the surface, always calm, cool, and collected, skillfully hiding his pain and suffering.

"Mr. Kumar, I don't want to sound insensitive to your pain and grief, but you were only seven years old. I am sure you did everything within your power to help him. Healthy people do overcome grief over a period of time, no matter how severe. It should not become a loop of suffering. It has been more than thirty years since your father died. Much has changed since that time. You are married now, have two beautiful children, a great job, and dreams," continued Dr. Joshi in an attempt to get a deeper understanding of Akash's point of view.

"I am not sure if you are telling the truth, at least, not the whole truth," insisted Dr. Joshi.

"Nothing has changed," shouted Akash. "I see my father's death everyday in Jhai ji's eyes, in her *white sari*, on her face without the *bindi* and *sindoor*."

"Tell me! How do you change that? How do you change that?"

No one had an answer. No one said a word. Not even

Dr. Joshi, with all her prestigious degrees that adorned the walls of her office, had an answer to Akash's questions. There was a complete silence in the room that was frequently interrupted by the sounds of sobs.

****

09 GIFT OF LOVE

Lying alone in the dark, unable to sleep, tossing and turning in her bedroom, Aarti ruminated over the day's events and wondered if Akash would ever forgive them. He kept uncharacteristically quiet and to himself on the way back home in the car. They sat together like strangers, as if meeting for the first time. No one said a word. No one knew what to say, perhaps, afraid of making the situation go from bad to worse. He did not even eat dinner and quietly went to his study room to lie on the couch alone. "Would Akash ever fully understand why we put him through such an uncomfortable position, causing pain and suffering? Would he ever understand why it was necessary?" wondered Aarti, as she lay sleepless in her bedroom.

"Is that what my children think of me? Is that what Aarti thinks of me after all these years we have been married? What made them think that way about me? What did I do to make them feel that way? How can my own family put me in such a shameful and embarrassing position in front of someone else?" pondered Akash as he rubbed his tensed eyes and temples, lying confused and hurt, alone in his study room.

Days went by, nothing seemed normal at home even though everyone pretended to act normally. Akash seemed exceptionally quiet and withdrawn. Aarti even had to cancel his next appointment until things settled down a little, but she knew she had to be strong and take Akash back to Dr. Joshi for therapy.

"How are you feeling?" asked Aarti, as Akash returned from work.

"I'm OK," he replied, in a terse, uncharacteristic tone.

"I have made an appointment for us to see Dr. Joshi for next week on Wednesday. Would that work for you?"

"What for?"

"Therapy," replied Aarti with the patience of a doctor.

"I don't need any therapy. I am fine."

"Listen, Akash; first of all I would like to apologize for what we said and how we behaved at Dr. Joshi's office. I know you are hurt, but not going to therapy is not the answer, and Dr. Joshi is our best hope. She cares about you and our family. She has been calling every day to find out how you were doing."

"I don't need any therapy. I am fine," repeated Akash, angrily.

"Yes you do! Don't pretend you are fine. Fine people don't take Ambien pills every night to go to sleep and Prozac every day to get up and go to work. Fine people don't collapse on stage because they can't control or confront their debilitating flashbacks, emotions, and demons. Fine people do not despair forever in grief over the loss of a loved one while negatively affecting other loved ones. Fine people don't abandon their motherland because they are too afraid to face the truth!" shouted Aarti. "I will not let you suffer like this any longer!"

"I said I was fine. It won't happen again, I promise," Akash tried to assure Aarti in vain.

"I am sorry, but there is no turning back now. You will go back for therapy with me if you love us. Don't do it for yourself if you don't want to, but please, do it for our sake," begged Aarti in an unflinching tone. "What has already happened we cannot change, but what is yet to happen we can shape and influence. At times, the first step is simply to break from the past and declare that it is you, not your history, who is in charge. Every moment you are alive, you can make new choices that help you move on and step toward a better future. If you pay attention to only mud on the ground after a storm, you won't notice that the sky above has already cleared. Don't focus on the mud. Make better choices today and move on," continued Aarti with passion in her voice.

"No, No, No! I can never forget Baoji. I loved him very much, I can never let go of his memories. How can you even ask me to move on? I had the best time of my life as a child with Baoji. He was a great father," said Akash with tears in his eyes.

"I will never ask you or expect you to forget Baoji. I wish he were still alive to see his daughter-in-law and his grandchildren. I would have loved him and respected him like my own father. But what you are doing is grieving, and suffering from neurotic guilt and shame, instead of cherishing his memories," argued Aarti.

"You don't understand; you won't understand because you weren't there," Akash tried to explain again his side of the story with a choking voice.

"Believe me, I know, life is not easy. We all know that. How we choose the way we think, feel, and act in relation to life's challenges can often make the difference between hope versus despair, optimism versus frustration, and victory versus defeat. With every challenging situation we encounter, ask constructive questions and put things in proper perspective."

"You should know better than anyone one else as a professor. Why do you think your students come to you for help when they are struggling with concepts?" challenged Aarti. "They come to you because they need help."

"Normal people have problems. The smart ones get

help," stressed Aarti before Akash could answer.

"But that's not the same thing. Mine is a different situation," defended Akash against powerful and persuasive arguments from Aarti.

"That's a matter of perspective," retorted Aarti.

"What do you want me to do? Spend the rest of my life in therapy that does not work? Put up with eccentric therapists, and go over and over my painful memories with them for which they have no medicine?" shouted Akash angrily.

"Can I ask you for a favor?" asked Aarti, full of hope in her voice as she came close and held Akash's hands.

"What is it?"

"How long have we been married?"

"It will be fifteen years in July, this year," replied Akash, with a perplexed look.

"I want you to come with me for therapy one last time with Dr. Joshi, and then let's all go to India for our wedding anniversary celebration. We have never visited India, or your ancestral home, ever since we have been married. We also want to visit the mountains that Baoji loved so much," asked Aarti, as her eyes welled up.

"Do you think you can give that gift to us?" asked Aarti, with teary eyes, while holding Akash's hands.

"Please?"

****

10 THE BRAIN ON LOVE

"Welcome back," said Dr. Joshi, as she greeted Akash and Aarti in her office a few days later. "I am proud of the courage you have shown by returning," she said, looking at Akash with appreciation.

"Before I begin, let me share the reasons why I asked your wife to join you in these therapy sessions. You see, in life we sometimes may feel we're walking alone, but we don't have to be, as long as we're honest with ourselves, and ask for help when needed," she continued after a short pause. "You can find strength and support through people you love and trust. Whether you speak Hindi or Chinese, people around the world use the same images of physical pain to describe a broken heart, which they perceive as crushing and crippling. It's not just a metaphor for an emotional punch. Social pain can trigger the same sort of distress as a stomach ache or a broken bone. But a loving touch is enough to change everything," pitched Dr. Joshi, with passion in her voice and animated hand gestures as she looked at Akash, who appeared tensed, for his approval.

"James Coan, a neuroscientist at the University of Virginia, conducted experiments in 2006 in which he gave an electric shock to the ankles of women in happy, committed relationships. Tests registered their anxiety before, and pain levels during the shocks. Then they were shocked again, this time holding their loving partner's hand. The same level of electricity produced a significantly lower neural response throughout the brain. In troubled relationships, this protective effect didn't occur. If you are in a healthy relationship, holding your partner's hand is enough to subdue your blood pressure, ease your response to stress, improve your health and soften physical pain. We alter one another's physiology and neural functions. During idylls of safety, when your brain knows you're with someone you can trust, it needn't waste precious resources coping with stressors or menace. Instead, it may spend its lifeblood learning new things or fine-tuning the process of healing. Its doors of perception swing wide open. Loving relationships alter the brain most significantly."

Akash listened carefully, and nodded in approval while Aarti sat next to him on the couch, holding his hand.

"I am recommending ten weekly therapy sessions in all, each lasting approximately sixty minutes, and each with a specific goal in mind," continued Dr. Joshi as she smiled at Akash, who appeared to be more relaxed now.

"Might there be more than ten sessions?" asked Akash.

"No," replied Dr. Joshi with a determined voice. "Studies have found most patients improve dramatically between their seventh and tenth session, and do not require therapy on a regular basis thereafter."

"But how can you be so sure of the results?" interrupted Akash, while holding back his inner excitement.

"I strongly believe in goals and outcome oriented therapy, and that patients should be able to graduate from it. I don't believe patients need to talk endlessly about how they feel or about childhood memories. I believe in aggressive therapy. I prod and assist my patients to face what they find uncomfortable: change."

"But not all patients are at the same level of illness or readiness for change?" asked Akash.

"No, they are not. You are absolutely right," smiled Dr. Joshi at Akash's eagerness to learn about expectations.

"Then?"

"Well, patients need a therapist's opinion, advice, and structured action plans. Popular misconceptions reinforce the belief that therapy is about resting on a couch and talking about one's problems. So that's what patients often do. And just as often this leads to codependence. The therapist, of course, depends on the patient for money, and the patient depends on the therapist for emotional support. And for many therapy patients, it is satisfying just to have someone listen, and they leave sessions feeling better. But there's a difference between feeling good and changing your life. Feeling accepted and validated by your therapist doesn't push you to reach your goals. To the contrary, it might even encourage you to stay mired in dysfunction. Therapy sessions can work like spa appointments: they can be relaxing but don't necessarily help solve problems. More than an oasis of kindness or a cozy hour of validation and acceptance, most patients need smart strategies to help them achieve realistic goals," stressed Dr. Joshi. She then pulled out two folders with complete details of each session, including homework, and handed them to Akash and Aarti to follow along.

Akash's eyes lit up with excitement as he reviewed the outline of each session carefully. He loved the idea of having structured sessions, each with a specific goal. Above all, he was thrilled to know that there was an end. He will be able to graduate like his own students, with pride. What good is a dream that comes true if you spend your whole life sleeping?" he thought.

"Homework?" asked Akash jokingly as he browsed through the folder.

"Yes, active participation by patients greatly improves their chances of achieving desired outcomes," stressed Dr. Joshi.

"I'm ready," replied Akash as he leaned forward.

"Good! I want you to take a few minutes and think of a goal you want to achieve at the end of therapy. Something you might have wanted to do, but have been afraid, or unable to do, due to your illness," said Dr. Joshi, as she readied to leave the office to give Akash some time to think.

"I already have," replied Akash before she could open the door.

"What is it?" asked Dr. Joshi as she turned towards Akash with a curious look.

"I want to visit India with my family for our wedding anniversary in July this year," replied Akash as he looked in Aarti's eyes. "I want to show them our family home. I want to show them the Himalayan Mountains that Baoji loved so much. I want to show them the pre-dawn sun paint the mountain peaks pink and purple, one at a time," said Akash as his eyes welled up.

"When was the last time you went to India?" asked Dr. Joshi.

"We have not been to India since Baoji's death."

"Wow! I think it's a wonderful goal. I am sure your family would love to hear about it," said Dr. Joshi.

"Please continue to take your medication and do your homework as assigned before our next meeting, and call me if you have any questions," replied Dr. Joshi as she moved to shake Akash and Aarti's hands.

***

"Thank you so much for everything," said Aarti, full of excitement as she gave Akash a big hug outside the office. "Are you going to tell everyone about your decision tonight?"

"Yes, I will," replied Akash in a calm manner as the two walked towards their car.

"Oh, I am so excited," said Aarti as she raised her arms

up in the air with joy. "This will be the best anniversary present ever."

Everyone at home was happy and excited to hear Akash's decision – happiness not seen since the Diwali celebration. Jhai ji thanked God with folded hands and blessed Akash by kissing his forehead in a customary fashion. She began reminiscing about their lives and home in India while Shreya discussed her shopping list with Aarti. Life seemed to have returned to normal, at least for now.

Akash slipped into his room quietly after dinner to review his homework before his next appointment. He pulled out the color coded folder labeled week one, and started to study. He was to set exercise goals and work up to the public health dose, which is 150 minutes a week of moderate-intensity exercise, or 75 minutes a week of vigorous-intensity exercise and fill out an exercise journal each day for the next ten weeks. Akash had made several unsuccessful attempts to exercise in the past. He was not fond of treadmills or boring walks. He enjoyed spending his free time at home with family or reading in his room. He knew he led a sedentary lifestyle, but it was hard to change.

***

"It's your life!" As with the general population, activity and exercise are very important for people living with mental illness," read the paper in the folder. "Many of these individuals are at a high risk of chronic diseases associated with sedentary behavior such as diabetes, hyperlipidemia, and cardiovascular disease. Exercise can have a huge impact on your health. Physical activity can lower the risk of early death, heart disease, and stroke, type 2 diabetes, high blood pressure, weight gain, and high cholesterol – all problems found among people living with mental illness. Exercises, including jogging, swimming, cycling, walking, gardening, and dancing, have been proven to reduce anxiety and depression. Studies show that exercise can have the same antidepressant effect as some traditional forms of treatment, including psychotherapy and group therapy. It also seems to have the potential for reducing anxiety. Just one session can result in at least a brief reduction in stress or anxiety, and regular exercise may have a long-term effect in reducing it. This can be particularly important for people who have mental health problems. They often have low self- esteem, partly at least because of the way society regards these difficulties.

"What are you reading?" asked Aarti as she walked in the room.

"My homework," replied Akash jokingly as he laughed. I am supposed to set goals for myself, exercise thirty minutes a day, and log it in the journal.

"So what's so funny about that? Even Dr. Johnson used to insist on doing the same."

"I know, but I did not have to fill out all this paper work with him."

"That's why you never followed through," retorted Aarti with sarcasm.

"You know I don't like exercising on a treadmill; it's so boring and it's too cold to walk or do anything outside. What am I supposed to do?"

"Let's walk together, indoors at the Briarwood Mall every day. We can even take the whole family with us on the weekends and start planning for our India trip while we walk. We will have fun and the time will fly by," suggested Aarti.

"I love that idea! Let's start tomorrow," replied Akash, brimming with excitement.

***

The first therapy session with Dr. Joshi went without much difficulty. Akash came in fully prepared with his homework, which included entries of the days, times, and duration of his exercises. Also included in the homework was a detailed list of triggers that caused anxiety. He discussed those triggers with Dr. Joshi and Aarti, though it made him uncomfortable at first. But it didn't matter anymore. He had already given his word to Aarti. He also learned ancient Indian yogas, like *Nidra* and *Samadhi* for relaxation and to overcome anxiety.

"While most people treat yoga as a body workout, the truth is that just as a car engine needs to be turned off to cool down after a long drive, yoga-nidra provides a deep restoration to your body and mind. The automatic symptoms of high anxiety such as headache, giddiness, chest pain, palpitations, and abdominal pain respond well to this yoga. Yoga-Samadhi, on the other hand, is a state of complete control over the functions and distractions of consciousness. Mind, body, and senses become steady, and in harmony in this yoga," explained Dr. Joshi.

"Self-awareness," preached Dr. Joshi in another session, is the greatest gift you can give to yourself, citing Gandhi to make her point. "As human beings, our greatness lies not so much in being able to remake the world—that is the myth of the atomic age--as in being able to remake ourselves."

"You can get a master's degree in practically anything nowadays, but where do you go to study you? You are the one subject that if comprehended on a Master's level, has the greatest potential to affect your long-term happiness and success. Self-awareness is to understand your personality, behaviors, habits, emotional reactions, motivations, and thought processes. Having more self-knowledge not only helps us make better choices, but also helps us understand our reactions to others. It is to move from shallow waters to the deeper end of the pool. Knowing why you think and feel as you do gives you access to information you can use to re-create your life."

Citing excerpts from Nassir Ghaemi's book, *A First-Rate Madness*, at yet another session, Dr. Joshi argued that most of us make a basic and reasonable assumption about sanity: we think it produces good results, and we believe insanity is a problem. This book argues that in at least one vitally important circumstance insanity produces good results and sanity is a problem. In times of crisis, we are better off being led by mentally ill leaders than by mentally normal ones. It is called, "The inverse law of sanity."

Four key elements of some mental illnesses —mania and depression — appear to promote crisis leadership: realism, resilience, empathy, and creativity. These aren't just loosely defined character traits; they have specific psychiatric meanings, and have been extensively studied scientifically. The author uses these terms in their scientific, not their commonsense meanings. Among these qualities, psychologists have studied creativity and empathy most, but resilience and realism are just as important for leadership and have also been examined in some detail by recent researchers. Of these four elements, all accompany depression, and two (creativity and resilience) can be found in manic illness.

Except for resilience, none are specific for other mental illnesses (like schizophrenia and anxiety disorders). Depression makes leaders more realistic and empathetic, and mania makes them more creative and resilient. Depression can occur by itself, and can provide some of these benefits.

"Bottom line," argued Dr. Joshi, "We are each gifted in a unique and important way. It is our privilege and our adventure to discover our own special light."

"Fathers really matter," elucidated Dr. Joshi during another session. "Mothers carry babies and create the environments in which they grow. But, biology is making it clearer by the day that a man's health and well-being have a measurable impact on his future children's health and happiness. This is not because a strong, resilient man has a greater likelihood of being a fabulous dad — or not only for that reason — or because he's probably got good genes. His children's bodies and minds will reflect lifestyle choices he has made over the years, even if he made those choices long before he ever imagined himself strapping on a Baby Bjorn."

Doctors have been telling men to eat right for years. What is unexpected are the psychological dimensions of epigenetics. Dr. Eric Nestler, a psychiatrist who did a discomfiting study on male mice and what he calls "social defeat." His researchers put small normal field mice in cages with big, nasty retired breeders, and let the big mice attack the smaller mice for about five minutes a day. If a mean mouse and a little mouse were pried apart by means of a screen, the torturer would claw at the screen, trying to get at his victim. All this subjected the field mouse to "a horrendous level of stress," said Dr. Nestler. This process was repeated for 10 days, with a different tormentor placed in each cage every day. By the time the torture stopped, about two-thirds of the field mice exhibited permanent and quantifiable symptoms of the mouse equivalents of depression, anxiety, and post-traumatic stress disorder. The researchers then bred these unhappy mice with normal females. When their pups grew up, they tended to overreact to social stress, becoming so anxious and depressed that they wouldn't even drink sugar water. They avoided other mice as much as they could.

In other words, what a man needs to know is that his life experience leaves biological traces on his children. Even more astonishingly, those children may pass those traces along to their children.

The change was beginning to take hold in Akash slowly.

Almost half way into his treatment, Akash finally began to appreciate the value of these therapy sessions. He especially appreciated Dr. Joshi's efforts to put a positive light on mental illness, and the fact that it was something treatable. He enjoyed intellectual conversations and respected her persuasive and cogent arguments. He did not even mind the drudgery of the homework each week. The winter chill that had descended upon their relationship at the beginning, due to her aggressive ways of confronting him, was beginning to change. Spring thaw was beginning to emerge, and he saw light at the end of the tunnel. But he also knew there was more to come. It couldn't be all that easy.

"Exposure therapy," as it was labeled, was their next and perhaps the most difficult session of the therapy thus far, as the three of them sat together in Dr. Joshi's office. In the safety of the office, while holding Aarti's hands, Akash made an mp3 tape, reliving what it was like to lose his father on that day, almost thirty years ago, as he sobbed. Akash was very brief at first in recounting the horrors of the accident that had haunted him since his father's death. But slowly, he mustered enough courage to recount in great detail, how the two had hiked, fully equipped with gear, ropes, and stakes. "We hiked through thick forest, dense woods, jagged rocks, and tea plantations to the top of the mountain. We walked directly into a rainbow-sherbet sky past a brood of waterfalls soaked in varied hues. The colors deepened and darkened, until the water transformed into molten silver and the nearby mountain range faded into a silhouette. We were in the midst of clouds. It was misty, serene, cool, and so beautiful that it felt surreal. The ground was still wet from the morning frost. My dad was so proud to be with me on top of that beautiful mountain."

But then, suddenly he slipped as he tried to move back a little from the rough, wet and slippery surface he was standing upon, and fell. He kept sliding down from the steep hill until finally he hit a huge rock that prevented him from falling. He tried so hard to climb back up, recounted Akash, "I threw a rope towards him so he could climb back up."

"What were you feeling?" Dr. Joshi asked.

"I felt helpless and started crying as I tried really hard to pull him back up. Then I don't remember anything after that, until the rescuers arrived the next day," replied Akash as he sobbed uncontrollably.

There was a long pause.

He then recounted how he felt dizzy and his heart raced with palpitations for weeks, even months after the accident. He was plagued by insomnia, and when he did sleep, he would have terrible nightmares of the accident. He became terrified of heights. He could not concentrate. He felt helpless, guilty, ashamed, and cut off from the people who were closest to him. He would hear his father screaming for help over and over, which would then set off a cascade of terrifying mental images, like a movie that he could not turn off. He would avoid anything that reminded him of that terrible day. He lost a piece of his life.

"These symptoms are the hallmark of PTSD," Dr. Joshi said at the end of the session.

She required that Akash replay the tape at home, daily. The goal was to show that grief and painful memories, like the tape, can be picked up or put away.

In the future sessions, Dr. Joshi asked Akash to recount his experiences over and over on tape again in the present tense, periodically asking him to rate his anxiety level on a scale of 0 to 100. She also taught him additional relaxation techniques to use in order to calm his body and mind when he became terrified. The idea was that with repeated confrontations with memories or situations that have even a remote probability of causing harm, the person actually learned and modified his expectations, and the level of anxiety went down.

Finally, she coached Akash on how to turn his nightmares into new dreams by using a technique called scripting, or dream mastery, which is a part of imagery rehearsal therapy which Dr. Krakow helped develop. "Nightmares can be a learned behavior," she told Akash. She then asked Akash to close his eyes and change his nightmare into a dream. A dream he truly wished had happened instead of the nightmare, and then he was to rehearse it until memories of the nightmare were tamed and the new dream took its place.

A relatively new field, called interpersonal neurobiology, draws its vigor from one of the great discoveries of our era: that the brain is constantly rewiring itself based on daily life, she told Akash. In the end, what we pay the most attention to defines us. How you choose to spend the irreplaceable hours of your life literally transforms you.

****

11 THE POWER OF ACTION

It was a gorgeous, sun soaked, crisp, and cool spring morning. The Kumar family had gathered at the Nichols Arboretum, fondly called the *Arb*, for the commencement ceremony arranged by Dr. Joshi to celebrate Akash's successful completion of therapy. It was a no small feat for Akash, who had been under psychiatric care for most of his adult life. The site chosen by Dr. Joshi also had a deep personal connection for Akash, for this is where he proposed to Aarti.

Ann Arbor is known as the city of trees, and this park is a testament to that reputation. Though most of the city is paved over and built up with commercial properties, in the middle of all that space there is a little oasis called the Nichols Arboretum -- a 123-acre site with panoramic views, and a path along the winding Huron River. Owned and operated by the University of Michigan and located on the eastern edge of its Central Campus, the Arb has extensive, but dispersed collections of native and exotic shrubs, masterfully crafted into a naturalistic landscape.

Wilderness reigns supreme and serene in this park, which is isolated by thick, lush green trees, hills, and valleys. It attracts students from the university nearby. Students often come here simply to escape the rush, enjoy the peacefulness of the park, and reconnect with nature. Beneath the shade of the abundant trees, students lie on blankets, doing homework, or just hanging out with friends. Children play, older people read, others canoe and kayak down the river. If nature had a happy hour, this place would sure be it.

The first greening of the grass is like the heralding of spring with that glimpse of brilliant green that soon grows to carpet the earth. Trees, warmed by the fresh sunlight and rain, begin to unfold their leaves until all trees have unfurled their finery. Many colorful flowers like snowdrops, crocuses, daffodils, forsythia, irises, juneberries, apples, and lilacs bloom in the spring. Each is beautiful in its own right; each marks another splash of color and life in the canvas of nature. There is something exquisitely lovely about walking through an apple orchard in full bloom in the spring. It defies description. There is the brilliant white beauty and gentle fragrance when the apples are in full bloom. Driving through the country during springtime, one sees fields of the iconic spring flower called the dandelion. They are far from the most beautiful flower. They are not dainty or exquisite, but there is some simple cheery vigor about dandelions which speaks to us about the heart of spring. There is some wild and unvarnished beauty to a field turned bright yellow by the endless profusion of dandelions.

It was a perfect day for an outdoor gathering. After congratulating Akash, Dr. Joshi asked Rohit to deliver a keynote address to mark this significant milestone in his Dad's life – a speech his mom helped write, and that he proudly delivered.

"Dear Dad, we are proud and fortunate to have a father like you. You are always there to help us with our homework or whatever is needed in our lives. We are glad that you went through with the therapy, because we need you, and we love you," read Rohit. "You have always taught us to take action because every story we have ever connected with, every leader we have ever admired, every puny little thing that we have ever accomplished is the result of taking action. We have a choice, you have taught us. We can either be a passive victim of circumstance or we can be the active hero of our own life. We are proud that you chose to be the latter."

"I want to share a story of determination, teamwork, devotion, and love, for this occasion."

"In 1883, a creative engineer named John Roebling was inspired by an idea to build a spectacular bridge connecting New York with Long Island. However, bridge building experts throughout the world thought that this was an impossible feat and told Roebling to forget the idea. It just could not be done. It was not practical. It had never been done before.

Roebling could not ignore the vision he had in his mind of this bridge. He thought about it all the time and he knew deep in his heart that it could be done. He just had to share the dream with someone else. After much discussion and persuasion he managed to convince his son, Washington, an up and coming engineer, that the bridge in fact could be built.

Working together for the first time, the father and son developed concepts of how it could be accomplished and how the obstacles could be overcome. With great excitement and inspiration, and the headiness of a wild challenge before them, they hired their crew and began to build their dream bridge.

The project started well, but when it was only a few months underway a tragic accident on the site took the life of John Roebling. Washington was injured and left with a certain amount of brain damage, which resulted in him not being able to walk or talk or even move.

"We told them so."
"Crazy men and their crazy dreams."
"It's foolish to chase wild visions."

Everyone had a negative comment to make and felt that the project should be scrapped since the Roeblings were the only ones who knew how the bridge could be built. In spite of his handicap Washington was never discouraged and still had a burning desire to complete the bridge and his mind was still as sharp as ever.

He tried to inspire and pass on his enthusiasm to some of his friends, but they were too daunted by the task. As he lay on his bed in his hospital room, with the sunlight streaming through the windows, a gentle breeze blew the flimsy white curtains apart and he was able to see the sky and the tops of the trees outside for just a moment.

It seemed that there was a message for him not to give up. Suddenly an idea hit him. All he could do was move one finger and he decided to make the best use of it. By moving this, he slowly developed a code of communication with his wife.

He touched his wife's arm with that finger, indicating to her that he wanted her to call the engineers again. Then he used the same method of tapping her arm to tell the engineers what to do. It seemed foolish, but the project was under way again.

For 13 years Washington tapped out his instructions with his finger on his wife's arm, until the bridge was finally completed. Today the spectacular Brooklyn Bridge stands in all its glory as a tribute to the triumph of one man's indomitable spirit and his determination not to be defeated by circumstances. It is also a tribute to the engineers and their team work, and to their faith in a man who was considered mad by half the world. It stands too as a tangible monument to the love and devotion of his wife who for 13 long years patiently decoded the messages of her husband and told the engineers what to do.

Perhaps this is one of the best examples of a never-say-die attitude that overcomes a terrible physical handicap and achieves an impossible goal."

Rohit paused for a minute as everyone clapped with teary eyes.

Gandhi once said, "You may never know what results come from your action. But if you do nothing, there will be no results."

"We love you Dad," said Rohit as Dr. Joshi handed a ceremonial diploma to Akash.

Feeling proud and moved by his son's loving words, Akash leaned forward with tears in his eyes and gave a hug and a kiss to Rohit as everyone clapped and joined in the ceremony.

****

12 HOMEWARD BOUND

"You must be so excited!" "You are so lucky!" "I wish I could go!" This is all the Kumar family had been hearing for weeks since they announced their trip to India. Friends and family were delighted to hear they were visiting their homeland for the first time in almost thirty years, and with every well-intentioned exclamation, nervous excitement kept building.

"Does India look like America, Daadi Ma?" asked Rohit, a history buff, as the Kumar family gathered to discuss their planned trip to India.

"Beta, even though India and America are in two different continents, both countries have a few similarities as well as many differences," replied Parvati. She went on to explain similarities such as how both countries were democracies, both were British colonies before their independence, both these nations had populations which were multi-ethnic with strong national patriotic pride. India and America were among the two largest countries in the world.

"What are the differences?" asked Rohit.

"Indian jewelry and clothes are so much better than American," interrupted Shreya quickly. "I have already made a long shopping list."

"All you care for is your shopping," retorted Rohit.

"And all you talk about is history. You are so boring," Shreya fought back.

"That's enough, children! No fighting," interrupted Aarti, before things got out of control.

"What else, Daadi Ma? You never answered my question about the differences," reminded Rohit with impatience.

Parvati explained how America was a relatively young country compared to India. America just turned 235 years old, while Indian civilization dated back around 5500 years. America was three times as large as India in size, but had only one third of its population. India was the second most populous country in the world with 1.24 billion people.

"I already know all of that from school, Daadi Ma, complained Rohit. "Tell me more about life in general in India."

"It will be very hot there, especially in New Delhi. It will remind you of the Arizona heat with humidity added on top of it," replied Parvati. "Be sure to pack extra sunscreen."

"Do you have a large house in New Delhi, Daadi Ma?" asked Rohit.

"Yes, we do."

"Who lives there now?"

"My sister and my brother."

"How come you never go back and visit them?" asked Shreya.

"Because I don't like to go alone."

"What else can you tell us about India?" asked Rohit.

"There is no traffic sense in India. People seem to snub all road laws, including traffic lights. Auto rickshaws, trucks, battered buses, occasional cows, dogs, and luxury cars, somehow all manage to creep onward. Drivers honk furiously as they move in and out of lanes, if there are any. We follow the rules and laws in America. America is clean. India is not. Pollution is throat-searing in India. Air is clean in America. America is one of the richest countries in the world and India is among the poorest."

"That does not sound very good; then why do you love India so much?"

Despite all its faults, explained Parvati, she loved India because it was still her country. She was born in India, and she got married in India. India was her motherland – mother India. She had many great childhood memories and friends there. People of India were nice, friendly, family oriented, full of energy, and colorful, among other things. She loved the delicious Indian food, colorful clothing, romantic movies, and great music.

"English is a widely spoken language in India. Most subjects are taught in English in India. India is ruled in English," she said, "but we laugh and cry in our own language – Hindi."

"I want to meet *Sharukh Khan*. He is so handsome and romantic. I love his movies. I wish I could marry him," said Shreya, in a romantic voice while running her fingers through her hair.

"Yea right, just like millions of other young girls, waiting to marry Sharukh. But we are not going to *Bollywood*," reminded Aarti.

"Why can't we Mom?"

"Ask your Dad."

"I thought the Indians were very smart people with so many doctors, engineers, and professors in India and all over the world?" interrupted Rohit with a confused look.

"Yes, they are," laughed Parvati.

"If Indians are so smart, then why is India so poor?"

"That one question perhaps is on every Indian person's mind, whether he or she is living in India or abroad," thought Akash as he listened to their conversation. That one question inspired Akash to write a book on this topic. It was a complex question to answer, and even more so for such a large and complex country as India. It is impossible not to be astonished by India. Nowhere on Earth does humanity present itself in such a dizzying, creative burst of cultures, religions, races, and tongues. Every aspect of the country presents itself on a massive, exaggerated scale, worthy in comparison only to the superlative mountains that overshadow it. Perhaps the only thing more difficult than to be indifferent to India would be to describe or understand India completely. India is the land of contrasts and contradictions.

Mark Twain, an American writer described India as...

> *"The land of dreams and romance, of fabulous wealth and fabulous poverty, of splendour and rags, of palaces and hovels, of famine and pestilence, of genii and giants and Aladdin lamps, of tigers and elephants, the cobra and the jungle, the country of hundred nations and a hundred tongues, of a thousand religions and two million gods, cradle of the human race, birthplace of human speech, mother of history, grandmother of legend, great-grandmother of traditions, whose yesterdays bear date with the modering antiquities for the rest of nations-the one sole country under the sun that is endowed with an imperishable interest for alien prince and alien peasant, for lettered and ignorant, wise and fool, rich and poor, bound and free, the one land that all men desire to see, and having seen once, by even a glimpse, would not give that glimpse for the shows of all the rest of the world combined."*

"Was India always poor?" asked Rohit again with even greater curiosity.

"No," replied Parvati, and then explained that India had a rich, glorious past. In fact, India had, not just one, but several golden ages. At the time of the fall of the Roman Empire in the west, and the European Dark Ages, India had a series of great flowerings of culture, both in the north and the south. India discovered the heliocentric universe, zero, and the circumference of the earth in astronomy during medieval times. India was the richest, most populous civilization in the world during the time of the Renaissance in Europe.

"Then what happened?"

"Times changed. India fell to outside forces," replied Parvati as her face turned solemn. She explained how India, a peace loving, prosperous, and rich country, saw successive invasions from Alexander the Great and Genghis Khan, to Tamburlaine and the British. They all ruled and plundered India for more than 500 years until its independence from the British in 1947. So much had changed during their rule. Early in 1947, before its independence, Mahatma Gandhi met Lord Bevin, the personal emissary of British Prime Minister Winston Churchill, in Delhi. Bevin said to Gandhi...

> *"Eighteen languages, 500 dialects, some 30 religions, a million gods and goddesses, 300 million individuals, infinity of castes and sub castes, and a population that is practically illiterate and half of which are beggars and thieves....Good luck, sir! Such a nation is ungovernable! It'd take you centuries to get anywhere!"*

"What did Gandhi ji say?"

"Gandhi ji wrapped his large white shawl a little more closely around him, and replied, "India has eternity before her.""

Akash excused himself and went to attend to other matters as the children continued their conversation with grandma for some time.

***

True to his nature, Akash planned the trip meticulously. After all, it was his wedding anniversary gift to his wife Aarti. He wanted it to be a memorable trip back home. He booked Air India's direct flight from Chicago to New-Delhi because Air India did not fly from Detroit, even though that meant taking a connecting flight from Detroit to Chicago. Akash wanted the children to experience Indian style hospitality onboard with Indian food and movies in executive class.

He took care of most formalities such as the passports, visas, and signing up for the Smart Traveler Enrollment Program with the State Department in case of an emergency. He took care of most of these formalities online, without much hassle, but no one can completely plan or avoid hassles faced at the airports due to threats of terrorism in recent years.

The 9/11 terrorist attacks have completely altered the airport experience in America. Flying is no longer a luxury, or even fun. In fact, it could be downright unpleasant. Airline security begins the moment you make your reservation and your name is checked against the Transportation Security Administration's (TSA) list. But the heavy scrutiny is done at the checkpoints. The chatty TSA screener initially checking your boarding passes by sweeping an ultraviolet light over your ID to be sure it's valid. They also may be trying to engage you in conversation as a way to detect any telltale nervousness or psychological issues. Anyone who has travelled can attest to standing in an airport security line shoeless, beltless, clutching a Ziploc bag and inching grimly toward a full body scanner. To avoid going through such a humiliating, though necessary process, Akash enrolled in government trusted-traveler security programs called the U.S. Customs and Border Protection's Global Entry and PreCheck. These programs expedite passenger screening and customs declaration processes for fliers willing to undergo rigorous background checks ahead of time for a fee.

The Department of Homeland Security has already spent $40 billion rebuilding or strengthening aviation security since the terrorist attacks of 2001. Approximately 45,000 professional screening officers have been hired by the federal government. More than 1,600 machines that function like a doctor's office MRI have been installed at airports nationwide to inspect checked baggage. Another 900 of the machines that scan carry-on bags at passenger checkpoints have been upgraded, to make it easier to find hidden weapons or explosives.

"But are we really safe?" thought Akash. "If so, then how did the Christmas day, underwear bomber, Umar Farouk Abdulmutallab, board a Northwest flight from Amsterdam to Detroit recently, despite such tight security measures? In 2011, a total of 1,320 firearms were found at checkpoints, many of them loaded. How many were not detected?"

More than 11 years after the September 11th terrorist attacks, it remains possible to use fake boarding passes to get through airport security checks, according to new evidence from security researchers and official documents published recently in the *Washington Post*. The security vulnerabilities could allow terrorists or others on no-fly lists to pass through airport checkpoints with fraudulent passes and proceed through expedited screening. They could even allow them to board planes, security analysts warn according to the report. The security gaps center on airline boarding passes, which can be issued up to 24 hours before a flight's departure. According to security researchers, the bar codes on those passes can be manipulated with widely available technology to change the information they contain: passenger identification, flight data, and codes indicating whether a passenger has qualified for expedited screening according to the report.

Authorities today still allow one-out-of-two international airline passengers to cross their borders without checking whether they are carrying stolen or lost travel documents. Currently, less than a quarter of countries perform systematic passport checks against Interpol's database, with details of 30 million stolen or lost travel documents. "These types of failures put lives at risk," thought Akash as he continued to complete travel arrangements.

Large and diverse countries such as India are especially

vulnerable to threats, warns the State department on its website. India continues to experience terrorist and insurgent activities which may affect U.S. citizens directly or indirectly says the website. Anti-Western terrorist groups, some on the U.S. government's list of foreign terrorist organizations, are active in India, including Islamist extremist groups such as Harkat-ul-Jihad-i-Islami, Harakat ul-Mujahidin, Indian Mujahideen, Jaish-e-Mohammed, and Lashkar-e Tayyiba. The U.S. government continues to receive information that terrorist groups are planning attacks that could take place in locations throughout India. Another prominent insurgent group in India is the Maoists (also known as "Naxalites"), informs the website.

"I am a rational person," thought Akash. "But incidences such as the Christmas Day Bomber and reports such as the one published in the *Washington Post* makes me worry and think twice about the safety of my loved ones."

Akash knew he had to rise above his fears and anxiety, just like a Lotus flower – the national flower of India. Anybody who has ever observed a Lotus flower emerging from a murky pond cannot fail to see the beauty of this exquisite plant. The flower always looks so clean and pure against the background of the dirty pond. Lotus flowers can grow in the filthiest water and unlikeliest places. Consequently, the gorgeous blossoms have come to symbolize the ability to rise above and face challenges.

After all of the worrying about security and planning he had to do for the trip, the day had finally arrived. Rakesh, a cardiologist and close family friend arrived with his wife Sonia at 8:00 am sharp as planned. After exchanging customary greetings, Akash handed them a large envelope containing their itinerary, copies of their passport, visas, and contact information in case of an emergency. Soon, everyone gathered inside the house for a quick prayer. Jhai ji distributed some sugar at the end as *prasad*, a customary ritual which symbolizes good luck.

"Let's get going now," said Akash as he headed towards the large van parked in the driveway under the sunny sky, though the morning was still cool. Both men loaded the luggage quickly while the ladies and the children sat in the van. Moments later, they were on their way to the Detroit airport – about half-an-hour away.

"You won't even recognize India," said Rakesh while driving. He was referring to the changes that have shaped the modern India in recent decades while the song *Yeh Jo Des Hai Mera* (This, my country) played in the background. "India has progressed so much," he touted proudly, as if he were showcasing his personal accomplishments. "So many Indians are now going back for better opportunities and to start new businesses," he continued. "I call it the brain-circulation (a term popularized by the news media and academia about people migrating in both ways)." It is often noted in the Indian news media that non-resident Indians (NRI's) as they are called, are even more patriotic than the locals. Rakesh was testament to that fact as he continued to share one happy story after another.

"Visitors often do not appreciate the complexity of the airports," interrupted Akash in order to bring everyone else into the conversation.

"Most of us have been to airports many times -- they are so familiar we may not pay much attention to them anymore," explained Akash. But if you go behind the scenes, airports are amazing mini-cities, providing services to all sorts of people and companies. Air travelers, airlines, private pilots and freight carriers all use airports in completely different ways. Perhaps no entity in the world juggles as many disciplines as a major airport: security, meteorology, technology, mixology, pipe-fitting, sharpshooting, sushi making, and more. At a typical large airport, over 100 million people can flow through in just one year. When you consider that the population of the United States is only 310 million or so, that's a pretty startling statistic!

"Airports are so different here than in India," said Parvati. "You see visitors roaming here inside the airports in huge numbers."

"I like to see the planes take off and land. It's so cool," said Rohit.

"I love to collect souvenirs from each airport when we travel, added Shreya.

"I just love to travel. It is so exciting to see different places," shared Aarti.

"Detroit Metropolitan Wayne County Airport (DTW) is one of the busiest airports in the United States and among the world's largest air transportation hubs," explained Akash as he looked at Rohit. It was also the highest ranking large airport in North America for customer satisfaction. This was his favorite airport in the country, because it was one of the newest, most operationally-capable, and efficient airports. It was also easy to drop off and pick up passengers from the airport. Welcoming more than 30 million passengers each year, the main terminal, finished in 2002, was spacious and full of light, with plenty of comfortable seats at each gate and a wide choice of restaurants. The airport had two new passenger terminals, 145 gates, six jet runways, and two modern Federal Inspection Services facilities for international arrivals and departures.

Their conversation soon ended as Rakesh pulled over to the curbside checking in front of the Delta Airline's terminal for a connecting flight to Chicago.

The whole area was packed and bustling with people travelling to their far flung destinations within America and abroad. People were trying to load and unload their luggage while others hugged their relatives and friends. It was a scene full of emotions. Full of smiles, hugs, kisses, flowers, tears, embraces…you name it. In the middle of all the cars pulling in and out, there were people of all ages, full of emotions, of tear filled goodbyes, longings of loved ones, of excited anticipation of arrivals. They could sense the excitement of people waiting to be flown to their far flung dream destination.

"The airport has to be one of the only places where true human emotions are portrayed," said Parvati as she got out of the van. "People may be depressed, sad, or stressed out while they are gone, but when they reunite with their loved ones after an absence, all that fades away with a mere smile or tear at the gate or the baggage claim of the airport. You can see people's worries and troubles disappear once they make physical contact with the person they have been waiting for. Those pure moments of bliss make everything feel alright no matter what their previous days were like," she continued her conversation with Aarti, while Akash and Rakesh quickly pitched in to help the skycap unload and check their luggage, and Sonia gave everyone a hug.

"Mr. Kumar, your luggage has been booked all the way to New Delhi. Your flight to Chicago is on time and will start boarding shortly at gate #3," informed the attendant in a blue jacket and a matching blue hat, as he handed the boarding passes to Akash. "Have a safe trip home," wished the friendly skycap. He smiled and pointed towards the gate.

"Have a safe trip everyone," wished Rakesh as he shook Akash's hand and hugged the kids.

The Kumar family slowly proceeded towards the gate as they waved at Rakesh and Sonia. Their journey had begun.

****

13 WHISPERS OF DEATH

The sci-fi writer and humorist Douglas Adams once wrote that no one uses the phrase "as pretty as an airport." He might have been thinking of Chicago's O'Hare International Airport, the second busiest in America. Coming from customer friendly Detroit's International Airport, it is like stepping into a different country. "People don't come to airports just to visit because airports aren't generally lovable places, but O'Hare has to top the list. The lines of irritated passengers, unfriendly staff, the noise, the confusing layouts, and the strange signs don't help your crazed dash through a mile-long corridor to make a connecting flight. It's probably nobody's favorite airport," thought Akash.

"Guess what?" said Akash while checking the Gate Guru App on his smartphone for the status of the flight and gate number.

"What is it?" wondered Aarti.

"The flight has been delayed for two hours. The departure time listed now is 4:45 p.m. instead of 2:45 p.m."

"Two hour delay?" shouted Shreya with disappointment on her face.

"I am so sorry beta, but these things happen. Let's enjoy our time together, instead. A few hours will pass in no time," said Akash. He was determined not to let anything spoil their trip.

"You don't seem to be surprised?" asked Aarti, looking at Akash.

"Honestly, I am not surprised at all. O'Hare is rated as the sixth worst airport in the country for flight delays."

"What are we going to do now? It is only 11:00 a.m. here," wondered Aarti as she checked her wristwatch.

"Let's have lunch first, and then we can decide," suggested Akash as he checked Gate Guru for points of interest in the airport. "Thank God I checked the flight status before going through security."

"Why is that?" asked Aarti.

"At least we have more options to choose from to make the delay more bearable," said Akash as he displayed a list of restaurants on his phone.

"I have an idea. How about if we eat Tortas Frontera and then see the Brachiosaurus skeleton, since they are both in terminal one?" suggested Akash.

"Yeah, I want to see the Brachiosaurus," replied Rohit, full of excitement.

"Mom, can we go shopping instead of seeing the stupid skeleton?" asked Shreya with a disappointed voice. "The Brachiosaurus skeleton sounds so boring."

"Sure, but let's have lunch first. I'm starving."

"Let's meet back here in an hour," said Akash as they proceeded in separate directions after lunch.

With almost four hours to go before the flight, Aarti and Shreya decided to browse a few stores for souvenirs to take to India, while everyone else decided to head to concourse B in terminal one to marvel at the massive Brachiosaurus cast skeleton, provided by the Field Museum.

***

"So how was it?" asked Aarti, as Akash arrived at their designated place of meeting.

"It was awesome, Mom," replied Rohit in an excited voice as he clinched and raised both fists in the air. "You should have come with us, mom; you would have loved it too."

"I know, but Shreya was more interested in shopping," said Aarti as they walked towards the gate after security clearance, where a sea of passengers, mostly Indians, waited for the boarding announcement.

"The security check wasn't as bad as they make it sound, was it?" wondered Aarti as everyone took a seat in Air India's Maharajah Lounge for first and executive class passengers.

"No! All that planning really paid off here," replied Akash, referring to the U.S. Customs and Border Protection's Global Entry, and PreCheck programs that he had enrolled in.

With a grand arched entrance fitted with scalloped sheer curtains, the executive lounge was tastefully decorated, befitting royalty. The hand carved hardwood furniture with cushions and tasseled bolster sets on a red carpet decorated the modern, eclectic lounge. On the far right corner was a sublime fountain made of dazzling marble with lotus shaped basins that were filled with rose petals and votive candles. On the left hand side corner of the lounge was a familiar statute of Maharajah, the official mascot of Air India. Maharajah had a distinct personality with an outsized moustache, striped turban, and aquiline nose. The symbol of graciousness and high living that had represented Air India globally. Akash remembered it all too well. It was the same airline he had arrived in as a child with his young father and mother.

It wasn't too long before two petite women in their 30's,

beautifully dressed in beige blouses and bright orange saris with black and white stripes, stepped to the podium. They made their first boarding announcement which everyone had been waiting for -- first in Hindi, then in English.

Soon, there was a long line of tired, but excited passengers, mostly parents travelling with their children to spend summer holidays. Everyone else waited impatiently for their turn. It was almost fifteen minutes before the next announcement was made for first-class and executive class passengers to board the flight. The wait had felt eternally long to the tired and weary passengers.

"Let's go," said Akash as he tried to wake up Rohit, while Aarti nudged Shreya.

"It's about time," said Shreya, showing her discontent with the wait as she stood up angrily. "What took them so long?"

"Come on, Grouchy," said Aarti, as she softly patted Shreya's cheek and gave her a hug. "Let's go."

After showing their boarding passes at the podium, everyone walked slowly through a short tunnel to the entrance of a huge, ivory colored plane with Air India's red and orange logo prominently displayed on it. The logo, a flying swan with conark chakra embedded in it, signifies vigor and advancement. Two air hostesses, dressed in beige blouses, bright orange colored saris with black and white designed stripes, and a traditional *Gajra* in their hair, welcomed them with their hands folded, their heads bowed and said, *"Namaskaar, Aapka Air India Mein Swagat Hai"* (Namaskaar, and welcome to Air India). There was the sweet smell of white jasmine flowers in their Gajra that permeated the air and cast a mysteriously welcoming spell.

The manner in which those two words, *Namaskaar* and *Swagat* were spoken by the air hostesses, reminded Akash of a Sanskrit verse taken from an ancient Hindu scripture, *"Atithi Devo Bhavah" (The Guest is God)*, which became part of the "code of conduct" for Hindu society. Recently it has also become the tag line of India's Ministry of Tourism's campaign to improve the treatment of tourists in India.

Everyone returned the greetings with the same politeness and gracefulness as the air hostesses. The most striking thing as they entered the executive class cabin of the gigantic 777-300ER jet was the sheer sense of space. The entryway was large; the windows were much larger than the conventional ones seen on 747's. The ceiling had been specially designed, and the cabin came with soft LED lighting. The cabin also had mood lighting, which helped create a pleasant atmosphere and was something useful to have when flying through different time zones on international flights. The children, however, were especially excited about the flat bed seats, also called sleeprettes. These seats, when fully reclined, were completely horizontal, creating a bed that was fully flat for comfortable sleeping during the 15-hour long, non-stop flight. Akash was able to select the quietest seats with the most leg room in the executive class, which were immediately behind the only row of first-class seats. Passengers were served their choice of stimulating cocktails and other non-alcoholic beverages upon arrival inside the cabin.

It was not until 6 p.m. that all the passengers were seated, and the cabin doors were closed. The flight finally pushed back from the gate and was airborne in ten minutes. The blue sky seemed reassuringly clear as the plane swept up over the water, coursing 14 degrees north towards Ontario. Chicago's skyline was shrinking and the light was turning to a yellow haze over Lake Michigan as the plane ascended toward an altitude of 35,000 feet.

Passengers were given a standard blanket, a duvet, and a large pillow. Passengers also received brand new socks, eye masks, and a Pierre Cardin amenities kit containing all sorts of luxurious toiletries. Meals were served shortly after take-off, on Royal Doulton's finest bone china collection. The meals featured an array of mouthwatering vegetarian and non-vegetarian dishes.

The seats were comfortable and upholstered in mustard-colored fabric with leather arms and headrests. The seats could be adjusted upright, reclining, or lie-flat. Seats were fitted with laptop power, and a large in-flight entertainment (IFE) screen. There was a huge selection of Hindi and English movies to choose from and keep everyone busy, but the Kumar family was too tired and therefore decided to unfold their seats and sleep after dinner.

The plane, carrying over 300 passengers and lots of precious luggage, was gliding smoothly through the clear blue sky -- thanks to the aircraft's state of the art system that senses turbulence and commands the wings control surface to counter it, thereby ensuring a smooth flight for the passengers.

***

"Didn't you sleep well?" asked Aarti, tapping Akash's shoulder, seeing that he was sitting upright in his chair.

"I did," replied Akash, while holding her hand against his face. "I slept for almost seven hours."

"These sleeprettes are so comfortable. I think the extra money spent on the executive class is worth the price, especially on long international flights."

"I agree. Look at the kids and Jhai ji; they are still sleeping," said Akash with a smile pointing towards the children, who were in the middle aisle with their grandma.

"Good morning, may I get you some tea or coffee?" asked one of the flight attendants with a smile, showing no signs of fatigue even after more than eight hours in the air.

"I will take some coffee with cream and sugar please," replied Akash.

"I will take some cardamom tea with milk and sugar please," requested Aarti.

"Air hostesses are so much more than a pretty face for the airlines," thought Akash with appreciation. "They do so much. Starting with welcoming the passengers with a smile when they arrive to helping them find their seats, fasten their seat belts and making important announcements during the flight. They take care of their passengers all through the flight and even during emergencies like the unheralded heroines of United Airlines flight 1549 that landed on the Hudson River. If it were not for their calm but direct commands for safe evacuation, God only knows what could have happened. But all 155 passengers made it out safely. Their jobs may not be as glamorous as they once were, but critical and underappreciated nonetheless."

"I'll be right back. I am going to freshen up," said Aarti as she moved her seat into an upright position.

"You know something," said Akash to Aarti as she returned and took her seat by the window. "I am really worried about how the children will cope with the throat searing pollution, especially in New Delhi. I can fly them home in luxury but unfortunately I cannot remove toxic air from the atmosphere for them."

"On the one hand, I am happy that our people are becoming wealthier by the day, but on the other hand, I am worried about the untamed motorization that is wrapping the cities in smog," continued Akash. "There are 20 million people in New Delhi already. I've read studies that show over 70% of India's surface water is polluted, and India's air is now the most toxic on earth."

"I am also worried about the road safety in India. We will be travelling from Delhi to Agra, and then Jaipur and states in-between by road," continued Akash with a grim look on his face. "India tops the world in road fatalities and has earned the nickname, 'the world's death capital.'"

"You worry too much."

"That's because I care about my family, about their health, and about their safety."

"So do I, but what can we really do?"

"That's exactly what I am worried about."

"Come on! Think about all the love and attention they will receive from their uncles and aunties. Think about the places they will visit and experience. Think about the majestic Taj Mahal and the towering Himalayan Mountains that they will see."

"But that does not solve the real problems."

"No, it does not. But then tell me something. What are you prepared to do?" asked Aarti. "We can sit here, complain, and worry all we want, but that does not solve these problems either, unless we are prepared to do something about it. What are you prepared to do?"

Their conversation was soon interrupted by an announcement from the captain, before Akash could answer.

> *"Ladies and gentlemen, we are currently flying over the Arctic Ocean at an altitude of 35,000 feet and cruising at a speed of 555 miles per hour. We will soon fly over Russia and continue our journey toward our destination via Kazakhstan. The current temperature in New Delhi is about 98°F or 36°C under hazy skies. The current time in New Delhi is approximately 2:45 p.m. and the arrival time is expected to be around 9:00 p.m. local time. We are expecting a smooth ride out to your destination. Your flight attendants will be serving breakfast shortly. Please continue to enjoy your journey."*

"They sure serve plenty of food," said Aarti, while pulling her food tray out.

"No kidding, I am still so full from dinner."

"Do you want to play some cards after breakfast?" asked Akash. "We still have six more hours to go in the flight."

"No, I feel like watching one of the Hindi movies," said Aarti. "That is an easy way to pass and enjoy three hours. I think the children are also going to watch a Hindi movie with Jhai ji. I just talked to them about it."

"No problem! I will go for an English movie instead, *The Untouchables*."

"Haven't we seen that movie already?"

"Yes, but I still love that movie. It is one of my all-time favorites."

Soon, the whole family pulled out their in-flight entertainment screen from their seats, and started to watch movies of their choice to enjoy or maybe just kill time. Frittering away a few hours from a 15-hour long flight without getting bored or losing one's mind was equally important.

"What are you prepared to do?" Those powerful words from Aarti and the movie reverberated in Akash's mind, as he rested his head on the back of his seat after the movie. "What are you prepared to do?" demanded the incorruptible, Irish American officer, Jim Malone (Connery) as he lay on the ground in a pool of blood from the gun shots. He had been shot as revenge for helping Bureau of Prohibition agent Eliot Ness (Costner), who was summoned to stop Al Capone (De Niro), who monopolized and sold liquor in Chicago illegally.

Akash slowly pulled the shade up from the window to take a look outside and had to cover his eyes from the glare. The sun was shining brightly, the sky was clear, and the weather looked pristine from inside the plane. There was barely a trace of clouds in the sky. Nothing seemed to be out of place. Everything looked picture perfect as the plane glided through the sky as smoothly as a swan on an unruffled lake.

"I will be right back," said Akash as he headed for the lavatory, located at the end of the executive class. The curtains were completely drawn, separating the executive class from the first-class and the economy class. As he walked by, he saw that most of the passengers were glued to their screens, perhaps for the same reasons – to kill time.

Suddenly, loud gun shots and screams rattled the plane, just as Akash reached for the lavatory door. The plane shuddered, shied, side-slipped, and skittered like a broken roller coaster at an amusement park. The smooth flying, state-of-the-art machine dipped, pitched, and dropped several hundred feet as if it had hit a slippery bit of sky and then slid as if over a churning waterfall. Its soundtrack was a cacophony of clattering tableware, falling laptops, gasping, and even crying passengers and crew members. Oxygen masks dropped from overhead as the jetliner took a harrowing drop. While some passengers sank into despair, struggling with jagged images of their near-extinction, others locked hands and prayed amid screams of terrified passengers.

The luxurious and smooth gliding flight from heaven had suddenly turned into a hellish nightmare, albeit only for a few moments.

"Akash!" screamed Aarti, as she tried to reach him unsuccessfully. Unable to reach the lavatory door handle, he lost control, fell, and started sliding toward the front of the plane.

"Aarti!" screamed Akash

"Dad!" screamed the children, as Akash continued to slide past them and through the curtains and hit his head against the cockpit door.

The fasten seat belt signs finally came on, followed by an announcement from Shalini, the head of the crew, who happened to be at the back of the plane.

> *"Ladies and gentleman, the captain has turned the seat belt sign on. Please return to your seats immediately, fasten your seat belts, and remain seated until further notice."*

Shalini then quickly called the captain for an update, but there was no answer.

The plane stabilized a few minutes later. Perhaps, the prayers of terrified passengers were heard.

"What happened?" screamed anxious and nervous passengers throughout the plane.

"Please sit down and remain seated," repeated Shalini. "We will give you an update as soon as we find out the details."

> *"Ladies and gentlemen," announced the captain in a feeble and shaken voice. "This is your captain. We apologize for the inconvenience. The situation seems to be under control at this time. However, please fasten your seatbelt and remain seated until further notice. We will give you a complete update in a few minutes."*

Shalini called the captain again from her service phone but received no information about the incident. Instead, he requested that they all look after the passengers and keep them calm.

Aarti ran towards the cockpit, disobeying the orders from the crew, only to find blood streaming from Akash's forehead as he lay unconscious. Next to him were scattered, dead, and injured bodies, and the cockpit door that was slightly ajar.

All of the crew members sprang into action, helping the injured, frightened, and traumatized passengers. One of the flight attendants, who had just served them coffee and tea, helped Aarti clean Akash's wounds and provide first-aid and some water.

Akash slowly regained consciousness and opened his eyes. Completely unaware of the situation, he asked Aarti, "Is everything alright? What just happened? Are the kids alright? Is Jhai ji alright?"

"Yes, they are alright," replied Aarti, with tears in her eyes and trembling hands as she hugged and helped Akash stand up on his feet. She tried to guide Akash away from the dead and injured bodies. She tried to walk him straight to his seat, but the destruction from the broken, scattered dishes, hanging oxygen masks, and terrified passengers and crew members was too much to hide as Akash looked around.

"What happened?" asked Akash.

"Nothing, let's just go to our seats. The kids are waiting."

"No, what just happened?" asked Akash nervously as his body started to shake as he looked around.

"Oh my God!" screamed Akash, as he saw dead and injured bodies everywhere behind him and panicked. His throat tightened as his heartbeat began hammering. The fear of a possible heart attack dominated his thoughts. Akash experienced a rapid heart rate that caused him to drop to one knee and clutch his chest. Feeling dizzy and sweating profusely, he tried to grab the handle of a seat nearby with sweaty palms as his knuckles turned white. He was overwhelmed with a sense of fear and dread that seemed unshakeable.

"No! Not now! Please not now!" screamed Aarti, as the flight attendant helped Akash sit on an empty seat nearby.

"Please Akash, please!" screamed Aarti, as she tried to shake him vigorously.

Aarti then abruptly ran to her seat and grabbed her purse filled with medications and sprinted back, just as quickly as she left. She then quickly pulled out two completely new medications, Propranolol, and D-cycloserine.

"Keep these two medications and give them only under severe and unexpected attacks," were the words of Dr. Joshi, recalled Aarti. "These two drugs are still in the experimental stages, though they have shown positive results under clinical trials. In a series of studies, people with PTSD who took Propranolol reacted more calmly on measures of heart rate and sweat gland activity. Participants who took an antibiotic called D-cycloserine, learned to override their fears far more quickly than those who did not," said Dr. Joshi.

Aarti quickly gave those two medications to Akash in prescribed doses. Aarti then instructed the flight attendant to help Akash with muscle relaxation, starting with his feet and working her way up, isolating, then squeezing and releasing each muscle. Aarti herself held Akash's hands and helped him with deep breathing.

"Come on Akash, come on! We can't die like this," cried Aarti as she pulled a family portrait in front of his eyes.

"You promised to show us our family home. You promised to show us the Himalayan Mountains that Baoji loved so much. You promised to show us the pre-dawn sun paint the mountain peaks pink and purple, one at a time."

"Remember, Akash? You promised to give us that gift for our anniversary."

Their efforts and prayers bore fruit, and Akash stabilized a few minutes later. His breathing returned to normal, pain subsided, and heavy sweating slowed down.

Relieved, Aarti then turned to the flight attendant and introduced herself. "Hi, I am Aarti and this is my husband Akash. Thank you for helping me save his life."

"Hello, I am Priya. It is my job and duty to help our passengers."

"I want to help you with the other passengers. I am a doctor in the U.S.," said Aarti as she pulled out her badge from her purse.

"What about your husband?"

"He seems to be stable right now. I am sure our kids and my mother-in-law can take care of him now. He will be alright," said Aarti, leaving their family portrait in Akash's hands as a source of strength.

****

14 FOUR HOUES OF COURAGE

Lying on the seat with his family's portrait resting on his chest, Akash's eyes opened slowly, exposing him to what seemed like an illusion. The darkness cut to a scene of pandemonium. The confusing and chaotic scene increasingly began to take on a sense of reality as his mind struggled to fully focus his consciousness on the circumstances. The scene gradually came into focus.

Aarti and two other members of the cabin crew were busy attending to injured and traumatized passengers.

Images of Mother Theresa flashed in Akash's mind as he saw Aarti and others, busy providing care with the utmost dedication. They were not worried about whether they would even live to see the plane land.

"They were the living examples of Mother Theresa," thought Akash as he tried to gather enough energy to stand up on his feet. Mother Theresa went into the slums when she didn't have to, and helped the poorest people in the world without selfishness and without any expectations of a reward. The words of Cardinal O'Connor pierced through his soul. In his sermon, the Cardinal used a story to summarize Mother Teresa's dedication. He recalled a diseased man, covered with maggots, whom he encountered on a tour led by Mother Teresa on one of his visits to Calcutta. He quoted the man as saying, "I have lived my life like an animal on the street, and I'm going to die like an angel, loved and cared for."

The Cardinal asked Mother Theresa what she had done. She answered, "I cleaned him, and I knew I was touching the body of Christ."

Akash's mind raced restlessly from one thought to another. Images of his father flashed in front of his eyes, screaming for help over and over, like a movie that he could not turn off; images of Rohit, proudly delivering the graduation speech. "Daddy you have always taught us to take action because every story we have ever connected with, every leader we have ever admired, and every puny little thing that we have ever accomplished is the result of taking action. We have a choice, you taught us. We can either be a passive victim of circumstance, or we can be the active hero of our own life. We are proud that you chose to be the latter."

"Will I ever be able to look in the eyes of my children and tell them my favorite story of courage?" thought Akash aloud as he grieved over his helplessness. "Will I ever be able to share the words of Julius Caesar (a coward dies a thousand deaths, and a brave man dies but once) without feeling ashamed of myself?"

The voices of Aarti and the Irish American officer, Jim Malone from *The Untouchables* screamed in his mind as if they were taunting him. "What are you prepared to do?"

"What are you prepared to do?"

"Is this it?" thought Akash. "Is this what I will be remembered for? Someone who was not able to save his dad or his family? Will this be my legacy?"

Brushes with death are often infused with a quality close to madness as the mind reels in the presence of death. It is crazy what people think about.

"Though my senses were deadened, not so my mind: its activity seemed to be invigorated, in a ratio that defies description," wrote Rear Adm. Sir Francis Beaufort, who fell off a boat in Portsmouth harbor on June 10, 1791, certain that he would drown.

Some people pray, others leap into action, and many report feeling a floating sensation. Yet it is the way the experience lingers in the imagination that may be most important, both for the immediate aftermath and for the months and years to follow. And while some sink into despair, struggling with jagged images of their near-extinction, for others the experience has an entirely different meaning.

With his family's portrait still in his hands, Akash cried with his head buried in his lap for a while, unsure on what to do. He finally mustered enough courage to stand up gently, and ask Aarti if there was anything he could do to help.

"How are you feeling?" asked Aarti.

"I am fine."

"The captain has not been able to make a contact with the ground controllers," screamed Priya over the deafening noise from concerned passengers. Everyone wanted to know the details. For the flight crew, each minute was becoming a stressful triage between keeping passengers calm and informed, which left them feeling guilty, exhausted and frustrated.

Amid the shouts, screams, chatter, and conflicting stories, Akash tried to sort things out and remain calm without jumping to conclusions.

"Are the pilots alright?" asked Akash.

"No," replied Priya in a hushed tone and shaky voice.

"The co-pilot, Mr. Yusuf has been killed," she continued, as she pointed toward one of several bodies by the cockpit. "The captain, Mr. Rana, is seriously injured. Your wife has already checked his vitals and provided the necessary care with what we have onboard."

"Has anyone informed the passengers as to what happened yet?"

"No, the captain has requested to withhold the information until he has made contact with the Indian authorities. Besides, it is already chaotic enough on the plane."

"May I please talk to the captain?" requested Akash in a loud and firm voice, so that Aarti could also hear him.

"I am a former commercial pilot," he continued as he looked at Aarti.

Shocked and surprised, Aarti hesitated for a minute, unsure about what to say, and then simply nodded in agreement.

"Let me clear it with the captain first," replied Priya, as she proceeded to call the captain on the service phone for an answer.

The cockpit door was barricaded after the incident with a trolley full of wine bottles to be used for defense in case of another attack. Two of the taller and more muscular male flight attendants stood nearby as guards.

A few minutes later, Priya returned with a nod of approval from the captain.

"I am not going to let my family and 300 other passengers die like this," thought Akash, as he entered the cockpit. "Yeh meri pratigya hai (This is my pledge)." He vowed to perish fighting.

"Mayday, "Mayday!" screamed the pilot in a frail and exasperated voice. "This is captain Rana, Alpha, India, flight 126. Do you copy?" Again and again, he screamed into the radio with desperation, but there was no answer.

"Hello," said Akash to the captain as he entered the cockpit. "I am travelling with my wife, two children, and my mother," he said nervously as he showed him his family portrait and travel documents.

"I trust you," said the captain. "I have already met your wife."

"Priya tells me that you are a former commercial pilot. What airlines did you work for and when?" asked the captain in a frail voice.

"I am not a former pilot, nor do I know how to fly. I lied."

"You lied? Why?"

"I am sorry, but there was no other option. Priya said that the co-pilot was dead and you were injured. I wanted to help for the sake of my family and the other passengers."

There was a long pause. The silence was frightening to Akash as he waited with baited breath for the pilot to respond. A few minutes passed, and then finally the captain broke the silence.

"I hope you learn quickly," said the pilot. "We don't have much time."

"Where is the nearest airport where we can land?" asked Akash.

"I have not been able to get a hold of any control tower," said the captain as he reset the transponder code in the cockpit to 7700, a code designated for emergencies.

"But you are severely injured, and still bleeding," argued Akash.

"I'll be alright," insisted the captain in a stern voice. "Besides, my daughter is getting married next week and I want to be there for her. I have brought some important gifts and jewelry for her wedding that she wanted."

"But we can't put the safety of our passengers at risk for the sake of her wedding, can we? We need to attend to the injured and needy as quickly as possible."

"There have been casualties on the plane, but I have been assured that no one else has been seriously injured. We can safely store the dead bodies in first-class until we reach our destination."

"But you are the most important person on the plane. Everyone's safety depends on you, and you are badly hurt."

"We don't have any other choice but to continue until we can make a contact with one of the en-route control centers. Planes can't simply pull over on the road, like cars."

"How will a control center know of our situation if we can't make a contact via the radio?"

"Aircrafts are fitted with transponders to assist in identifying them on radar and on other aircraft's collision avoidance systems. It is an electronic device that produces a response when it receives a radio-frequency interrogation from the ground based control system. That's how the controllers can identify a plane's location, altitude, and speed on the radar. These transponders are set to an assigned code for identification."

"What happened anyway? How did these people die? What were those gunshots about?"

"Two passengers sitting in first-class tried to hijack the plane. They tried to force their way inside the cockpit at gunpoint as one of the flight attendants tried to serve us coffee. My young co-pilot and the flight attendant fought back, and the shootout ensued. Two other members of our backup team, sitting in first-class were also shot as they tried to help. Both hijackers and four members of our crew died."

"Aren't the pilots trained to cooperate with the

hijackers?"

"Yes we are, but our crew decided otherwise. They fought back instead and saved the plane and its passengers from going into the hands of hijackers. Who knows what would have happened? They were brave people."

"Let's not waste any more time," ordered the captain. "Let's get to work on your training."

The crash course in flying started immediately, with the pilot showing Akash all the instruments that must be monitored. He also handed Akash two big, bulky black bags that contained reams of reference material needed for the flight. These bags contained in them: the aircraft's operating manual, use of avionics, safety checklists, logbooks for entering airplane performance data, navigation charts, weather information, airport diagrams, critical details about how planes work, fly, take off, and land.

The captain then shared with him a few important lessons learned from others' mistakes. When an airplane stalls in the air and starts to nose dive, a phenomenon called *aerodynamic stall*, it is a natural instinct to pull back on the control stick and drive the plane's nose higher – a move that only exacerbates the problem. That was the leading reason why Air France flight 447 plummeted almost 38,000 feet in four minutes before hitting the water and killing all 228 people aboard in 2009. It was the same mistake pilots made on the Colgan Air crash near Buffalo, New York, that killed 50 in 2009. Learning to overcome that impulse, and instead to maneuver the nose toward the ground to regain speed is critical. It is just like steering your car in the direction of the skid during hydroplaning.

He then instructed Akash not to use any electronic devices in the cockpit as they can not only interfere with the avionics, but also cause distractions. It's akin to texting while driving.

Intense mental focus, self-control, good judgment, intuition, and extraordinary concentration are needed as a pilot.

Take for example; Captain Sullenbeger of US Airways Flight 1549: his plane suffered a double bird strike, and lost power in both engines. He watched the dials show thrust slipping away shortly after takeoff. The controller instructed the pilot to land at the nearby Teterboro airport in New Jersey. Instead, the pilot used his intuition, and told the controller that they would ditch the plane in the river. What might have been a catastrophe in the densely populated city of New York — one that evoked the feel if not the scale of the September 11 attack — was averted by a pilot's quick thinking and deft maneuvers which later became known as the "Miracle on the Hudson."

That's the difference between a massacre and a miracle.

"Were any parts of the plane damaged that we know of?" asked Akash.

"I can't be 100% sure," replied the captain. "I have not been able to make contact with any of the control towers. I am not sure if the communication system is simply not responding temporarily, or if there is permanent damage. We will know more as we go and when we are ready to land. Landing could be very tricky if any of the equipment is damaged. But the most important thing is that all of the windows, the windshield, and the pitot probes (tubes) did not break during the shootout. Damage to any of these areas could have had catastrophic consequences."

"What are pitot tubes?"

"Pitot tubes are small cylinders that sit outside the body of the plane to calculate airspeed," he explained. The captain then explained that the importance of these tubes would be hard to overstate. Without them, a plane's flight computer has no way to determine speed, and the automatic pilot shuts down. The plane will suddenly revert to manual control, forcing pilots to take the stick of a half-million-pound aircraft.

"In theory, this shouldn't cause a crash," he explained. The probes can be compared to a speedometer in a car: steady on the gas, and you'll be fine. Pilots are trained to respond to pitot failure by maintaining pitch and thrust until the probes resume working. Most of the time, they do. But during the period of manual control, the margin of error is thin. For a passenger jet like this one, the ideal cruising speed is about 560 miles per hour. If you go much faster, the center of lift moves back on the wing, pushing the nose down and increasing velocity, until you soon approach the speed of sound. At that point, shockwaves develop on the wings, interrupting the flow of air and reducing lift. The nose of the plane then gets forced into a dive that the pilot may not be able to pull out of. Then again, if you go too slow, the airplane stalls and falls. A plane must maintain a minimum speed to generate lift, and the higher it travels, the faster it must go. At 35,000 feet, the gap between too fast and too slow narrows ever closer. Pilots call it the "coffin corner."

"Whew! Thank God for that," said Akash nervously, wiping sweat off his face.

"Do you still want to help?" asked the captain with a smirk on his face.

"Not if we could all take the bus instead."

"Well, that's not happening, so get busy with your reading and ask questions," said the pilot with a forced smile, as he rested his head on the back of his seat and closed his eyes. Within a few minutes, the exhausted and frail looking pilot, still covered in blood, drifted off to sleep as Akash looked on worriedly and prayed. Akash's mind was running wild like a race horse, filled with anxious thoughts. Trying to focus one's attention under these circumstances can be challenging, if not impossible, but focus he must, thought Akash as he tried to regulate his thoughts on a straight course. His eyes fixated on the aircraft's operating manual as he pored over the reference material.

Suddenly, the unexpected sound from the cockpit's radio startled Akash. It was the airport operations control center (AOCC) at Indira Gandhi International Airport (IGI) in Delhi, where more than ten senior officers huddled in a room fitted with state of the art large screens and radars.

"Hello, Alpha, India, 126. This is the Delhi operations control center. Do you copy?"

The radio blared again as Akash tried hard to control his first instinct to answer the radio. Instead, he pulled the radio out and put it near the captain's face as he shook his shoulder.

"Captain Rana!" shouted Akash. "Please answer the radio."

"Hello, Alpha, India, 126. This is the Delhi operations control center. Do you copy," repeated the person in a tensed voice.

Slowly, the captain opened his eyes, grabbed the radio and answered laboriously. "Yes, I copy. This is Alpha, India, flight 126."

"We were contacted by the Kazakhstan area control center. They were unable to make a radio contact with your plane and informed us that your squawk code was set at an emergency level."

"What is your assigned squawk code?" asked the controller.

"0456," replied the captain.

"What is your current code?"

"7700"

"Please reset your squawk code to 0457 so that we may identify you on the radar."

The captain followed his instructions and reset the code on the transponder as ordered. He was barely able to keep his eyes open as he waited for further instructions with his head rested on the back of his seat.

"What is the nature of your emergency?" asked the

controller, a few moments later, after spotting the flight on the radar.

The captain then slowly explained the situation in a voice that was barely audible and was asked to repeat several times for clarity, as the captain's condition deteriorated quickly.

The captain then turned to Akash and asked for a favor in a fading voice with his eyes closed and hands trembling.

"What is it," asked Akash nervously.

"Will you please do *Kanyadaan* for my daughter if something happens to me?" implored the captain in a frail voice, handing Akash the picture of his daughter, Veena.

"Please, captain. Don't say that. Nothing is going to happen to you," said Akash."

"Who said that I was going to die?" whispered the captain. "I just wanted to be sure that someone…" said the captain, as he collapsed to the side without being able to finish his thoughts.

Akash quickly reached Priya and Aarti on the service phone and requested urgent help.

"Call the minister," screamed one of the officers at the control center referring to Mr. Singh, the minister of civil aviation of India.

Thick, off-the-scale smog shrouded New Delhi, the capital of India, as the temperature soared to over 40°C (104°F). Otherwise a colorful and vibrant city, the scene was colorless as street lamps and the outlines of buildings receded into a white haze. The combination of heat and dust had reduced the visibility to below a few yards. This summer so far had been the hottest since 1980, with an average maximum temperature of 41.57°C (107°F). As many as 49 of the 61 days in this two-month period saw the mercury soar past 40°C, another record for the past 33 years.

Televisions in the operations control center, normally tuned to NDTV, were switched to CNN international, as the news of AI flight 126 broke out.

"How the hell did they find out about this?" screamed one of the senior officers. "Now we will have to deal with the press on top of this mess."

"Kazakhstan authorities, maybe," speculated another officer standing nearby.

"The minister is on his way," announced another officer as he hung up the phone.

By the time the minister's car arrived, the operations center building was already packed with reporters waiting for updates. Many other news channels had started to broadcast live updates on the story and the whole nation became glued to their televisions.

The minister was escorted swiftly past the crowds and reporters into the building where several senior officers were already gathered and were discussing their options. A special hot line was established to handle the crisis, connecting the operations center with the defense ministry, and home ministry of India. Both, the Chief Minister of Delhi and the Police Commissioner were also summoned to the meeting.

While the high level talks to deal with the crisis were taking place at the control center, Priya, Aarti, and two male flight attendants helped move captain Rana, who was unconscious, to a seat in first class that had been unfolded, flat.

Akash quickly moved to the pilot's seat while Priya took the co-pilot's seat and called MedAire, a company that provides cabin crews with medical advice. The company soon determined that the case was too serious as it would require a surgery, and referred the case to a specialist at the Mayo Clinic. Within minutes, a surgeon was on the phone with Priya in the cockpit to help Aarti perform a surgery on the captain. Fortunately, Aarti was carrying enough basic medications like nitroglycerine, antihistamines, prednisone, sedatives, and painkillers with her, just in case someone needed them in an emergency.

A communication chain was hurriedly established in the plane. Aarti talked to the flight attendant, who talked to Priya in the cockpit, who talked to the surgeon and received instructions that were relayed back using the same chain.

Back at the operations control center, the decision was made to bring the flight back to New Delhi because it would take as long to divert the plane as to reach their destination. Also, no other airport in the area was as well-equipped as the one in Delhi.

While the operations control prepared for their part, the aviation minister went outside to provide an update to the reporters who had been waiting anxiously along with the rest of the country.

"No," yelled the former Air India pilot Irshad Fahim, who had been watching the breaking news story at a restaurant to beat the summer heat in Connaught Place -- the heart of New Delhi's business and entertainment hub. "This is too risky."

Irshad then quickly called a close friend at the control tower and asked if he would convey to the pilot that the decision to land at the IGI airport in Delhi was too risky due to the poor visibility around the area. The risks involved in landing a plane in a hugely densely populated area in case of any malfunctioning of the equipment were too high. Instead, he recommended that the plane be landed at the abandoned airfield of the Indian Air Force (IAF-Fields), located near a village, just a few miles outside the city. He volunteered to guide Akash to land the plane there safely, as long as his plan was approved and material support was provided by the ministries of home and civil aviation. He then gave a list of things he would need in order to accomplish his plan, as he rushed to the airport in his car.

After some hesitation, the controller agreed to convey Irshad's message to the new captain – Akash.

While driving to the airport, Irshad quickly called his son Faisal and daughter Zoya and discussed the plan of action with them and sought their help.

Akash discussed Irshad's suggestions with the AOCC and insisted that Irshad be included in any plan – something they agreed to reluctantly.

It wasn't long before Irshad arrived at the AOCC and presented his plan in detail to the ministers and senior officers.

"This is a ridiculous and a dangerous plan," said Mr. Singh, the aviation minster, to Akash, of Irshad's plan. The minister insisted on his own plan to land the plane at IGI. He bragged about the state of the art equipment and other resources available at the airport there. "We can land the planes here even under low visibility, using a procedure called the CAT IIIB landings. The procedure uses a combination of radio signals and high intensity runway lighting to land planes under severe conditions."

"Don't the pilots have to be trained and certified to perform CAT IIIB landings?" asked Akash.

"Yes, they do."

"But you already know that I am not even a pilot, let alone a certified one, and the real pilot is incapacitated."

"The other option is much worse. The other airfield has not been in use for years," added the defense minister, Mr. Rathore. "We don't even know if the control tower equipment is still operational. The runway is too short for such a huge plane, and I'm sure it is full of potholes."

"Those things can all be fixed quickly. We still have enough time if we all hurry and follow my plan," argued Irshad passionately. "We can land this bird, even on a short runway. It will be a hard landing, but it can be done. It is still safer to land there because the runway is surrounded by open fields."

"Do you have a family Mr. Fahim?" asked Akash.

"Yes, I do. I am married, and we have two beautiful

children named Faisal and Zoya. Both of them are students at Delhi University."

"How important are they to you in your life?"

"I would sacrifice my life for them in an instant."

"Which plan would you choose if your family was in this plane, and why?"

"I would still choose my plan over theirs without any hesitation."

"What makes you so confident?"

"I have flown planes for Air India at home and abroad, including the one that you are flying, for more than ten years without a single incidence."

"Why are you not working for Air India any longer?"

"I was fired for being an outspoken critic of Air India on its safety and service record. Billions of rupees of hard earned public money was being lost and wasted. The airline had become a source of shame due to embarrassing incidents like the midair scuffle between pilots and flight attendants during which the plane was reportedly unmanned for a few minutes. Then there was the flight to Toronto that was delayed for eleven hours while staff searched for rats that had climbed aboard the plane. On another occasion, a pilot was in the news for covering the windows with newspaper to keep out the sun. I was sick and tired of the impotent and ineffective bureaucracy of a state run enterprise. I had become a thorn on their side."

"He is nothing more than a fired and angry pilot who holds a grudge and is trying to settle the score with the state by taking advantage of the crisis!" yelled the minister of aviation.

The words of the late Steve Jobs, the former CEO of Apple, flashed in front of Akash's eyes as he mulled over the two conflicting plans.

"You can't connect the dots looking forward; you can only connect them looking backwards. So you have to trust that the dots will somehow connect in your future. You have to trust in something -- your gut, destiny, life, karma, whatever. This approach has never let me down, and it has made all the difference in my life."

Akash then thought about Captain Rana's advice, that intense mental focus, self-control, good judgment, intuition, and extraordinary concentration are needed as a pilot, and how those qualities changed an outcome from what could have been a massacre, to a miracle on the Hudson.

Akash felt some kind of connection with Irshad. The connection was trust. He was witnessing a private and personal moment. He felt connected to everything Irshad had to say. Maybe it was his goodness. Maybe it was his courage. Maybe it was the way he cared about the situation and fought his way in the room. Maybe it was magic or something like that. But it felt as real as the stars in the sky.

"We will land the plane at IGI, Delhi. That's the final decision," said the home minister, Mr. Yadav with authority. "We can't risk everyone's safety by landing anywhere else."

"What safety are you taking about, Mr. Yadav?" roared Akash, like an injured tiger. "Do you know that more than 135,000 Indians are killed on the roads every year? Do you know that India is nicknamed as the death capital of the world? Do you know that India has the dubious distinction of being number one in the world in road fatalities?" Do you know that almost 400,000 Indians die each year in preventable accidents like in rails, stampedes, buses, building collapses, and traffic fatalities?

"Yes, I do know!" said Mr. Yadav angrily.

"Well then, tell me something. Why should I trust you with that kind of safety record?"

"The minister of road and transport is aware of the problem and is working diligently to address those issues."

"Address those issues? How? If he is addressing those issues, then how come the problem has been getting progressively worse instead of getting better? How many Indians must die before something is done?"

"It takes time."

"No! It takes courage, it takes vision, and it takes commitment."

"Have you ever heard the name of a little boy Janpeet Singh?" asked Akash.

"No, I don't recall."

"Janpeet was a four year old boy, who was crushed under a school bus and died in the arms of his eight year old brother, Parmeet. His books were scattered on the ground next to his crumpled body when his grandfather came to pick him up from the school bus. I have Janpeet's picture hanging in my office with his distressed father, Arvinder Singh. Maybe you should too. I see them every day in the office and cry. Their images haunt me. He could have been the Prime Minister of India someday, just like Man-Mohan Singh."

There was complete silence on the other end. No one said a word.

"How long would it have taken you to fix the problems if he was your son?" continued Akash, after a short pause.

"India's air is now the most toxic on earth, killing many more, as if winning the dubious distinction in road fatalities wasn't enough."

"One day, I am afraid, the children in India will be singing 'Twinkle, Twinkle, Little Star,' without even knowing what stars are, if nothing is done to correct the problem."

"You are insulting India and its people," chided the minister. "India has progressed so much. India is one of the fastest growing economies in the world."

"Economic growth on the dead bodies of the innocent and poor should not be a source of pride for anyone."

"We don't need a lecture on what to do from some angry and arrogant *NRI*, (Non-resident Indian)."

"You are not used to being challenged, Mr. Yadav. You are used to people standing in line outside your door, and saluting you, calling you *My Baap* (Dear Sir, My Caretaker). We were slaves to the British before independence; unfortunately, we have now become slaves to our own politicians. I am angry, no doubt, but not arrogant. I am angry because I love my people. I am angry because I care about my country. And finally, yes, India is one of the fastest growing economies in the world, but that is not because of you, but rather in spite of you. It could be the fastest growing economy in the world if only the government would get out of the way of its people."

"We are losing precious time," reminded Mr. Singh, the aviation minister. "We need to clear the skies and start preparing for the landing."

"We are not landing at IGI, Delhi. We are going to follow Mr. Fahim's plan and land at the abandoned airfield of the Indian Air Force."

"Are you sure, Mr. Kumar?" asked Mr. Singh.

"Yes, I am sure."

"Mr. Kumar, we will provide full support as per your plan, but you will be held accountable for any criminal charges under the constitution of India, for endangering the lives of passengers."

"Allow us to land safely first. I will worry about the rest when the time comes."

"Arrest him upon landing for endangering the lives of passengers and insulting the state of India," ordered Mr. Yadav, the home minister. "That is, if he can even land."

"Yes Sir," saluted the Police Commissioner, Mohammad Rashid, as he exited the conference room.

****

15 MIRACLE IN THE FIELDS

"We are wired to be inspired," writes Jonathan Haidt, a psychologist. The sight of one stranger helping another in the out-of-the-blue fashion like Irshad can move people to tears. Acts of courage and compassion have a special psychological potency for most people, moving them or even thrilling them. He uses the term "elevation," to describe such a feeling. This feeling is so special that the Japanese even have a special word for it: *kandou*. True compassion means not only feeling another's pain but also being moved to help relieve it. Those who feel another's distress most strongly are most likely to help; those less moved can more easily ignore someone else's distress. Mr. Haidt found that elevation was contagious. Merely hearing about a heroic or altruistic act can stir the impulse to perform one in turn. That may explain why cultures everywhere have retold stories of heroes performing courageous and kind deeds, he explained. The police commissioner himself was *elevated* in that sense.

The commissioner urgently reached his deputy, Mr. Gupta, at his home, while he was being driven to the police headquarters soon after the meeting. The commissioner assigned the task to lead efforts for what was dubbed *"Operation Pratigya,"* to his deputy, with complete authority.

Within minutes of the order, a flotilla of police cars with blaring sirens and flashing red lights, was escorting more than twenty cars and trucks heading to the airfield. While being escorted, Irshad feverishly worked the phone, giving instructions to his son, daughter, and others who were following closely behind. The entire scene was being broadcast live on all national television networks through cameras mounted on the trucks that followed. The whole country was transfixed to their televisions to witness the landing that seemed surreal; it was more like a scene from an action film.

Sitting alone in his office, the police commissioner pondered the orders to arrest Akash. Shallow emptiness consumed his mind as he thought about Akash and Irshad. Darkness loomed within him about how he had accepted the orders from the minister and saluted to his authority without any thoughts. The story of Janpeet Singh pierced through his heart and soul as he looked at the pictures of his own children. "It was happening every day in India," he thought. "But nothing of any consequence was ever done. Akash was right. We don't value life here in India. We are all guilty. We are part of the problem because we are the system." Such thoughts continued to haunt the commissioner. Unable to carry the weight of his own guilt and shame, the commissioner gathered just enough courage to write and sign two documents. He faxed one copy to the deputy commissioner's office and left the other on his desk. He then removed his badge, hat, belt, service gun, and locked them in a safe with a note. Finally he called his home and asked for his personal car and driver be sent to pick him up.

The driver opened the car door and saluted the commissioner as they arrived home, and as always, the commissioner acknowledged the driver by bowing his head softly, but without making eye contact.

"You are used to people standing in line outside your door, and saluting you, calling you My Baap. We were slaves to the British before independence; unfortunately, we have now become slaves of people like you." The words of Akash pierced through the commissioner's mind, as he walked towards the house.

Suddenly, the commissioner turned around and asked the driver his name without making eye contact.

"Shyam Singh, Sir," replied the driver.

"Kitne saal se kaam kar rahe ho yaha par?" (How long have you been working here?)

"Pacchis saal se, sir." (Twenty-five years, sir)

"Kaha ke rehne wale ho?" (Where are you from?)

"Rampur gao se hein sir." (I hail from Rampur village)

"Biwi aur Bacchey?" (Wife and kids?)

"Wo sub gao mein rehtein hein, sir. Mein har mahiney milne jata hu or paise bhejta rehta hu," (They all live in the village. I go to meet them once a month and send money regularly)

The commissioner didn't say a word. The reality of Akash's words was starting to sink in. With his head lowered, he rubbed his forehead as his eyes filled with tears that he hid skillfully. He then quietly walked inside the house, pulled some money out of the safe, and asked his wife to give that money to the driver and tell him to take a few days off and bring his family back with him.

"Much had changed in India since independence, but much had remained the same," thought the commissioner. The country was slowly moving away from a caste-based to a class-based society. The social and economic mobility still remained limited, especially for the less educated, and under privileged. It was the product of India's layers of cultural legacies: the Hindu caste system, the feudal hierarchies established by its many invaders, and the imperial bureaucracy imposed by Britain.

"Is everything alright?" asked the commissioner's wife when she returned.

"Yes, everything is alright."

The commissioner then held her hand and together they

walked to the room where the family regularly prayed in front of the Quran, which was neatly wrapped in green silk, and kept on a pedestal. There he announced, "We will all go to the Mecca for Hajj this year."

Taken completely by surprise, his wife looked into his eyes as if she did not believe what she was hearing. She knew her husband was not a religious person. He did not even perform Salat (Namaz) five times a day as required of all Muslims.

"I thought you did not believe in Allah" said his wife, with suspicion.

"I will believe in any one or any power that will land the plane safely today."

"Which plane? What happened?"

He walked her to the family room and turned the television on for the latest news.

***

Gandhi was probably one of the most ardent fans of the Indian villages when he said, "The soul of India lived in its villages." India is still essentially a very large village. Sky-kissing condominiums and ritzy multi-level malls may be the order of the day in rapidly changing Indian cities, but the real India still lives in its villages.

The clarion call came to the villagers of Mahan shortly after 9:00 p.m. through the loudspeakers of their temple, followed by one from the *gurudwara*, and another from a mosque. Shortly thereafter, the church bells joined in the chorus. The village, Mahan, belonged to a new India: it was neither rural nor urban but something in-between. The village, about an hour drive from New Delhi, was one such island in a rural sea, surrounded on all sides by swaying grass, wooden buffalo carts, and diligent farmers working in the fields. Hundreds of villagers -- men, women, and children were marching towards the airport within minutes of the call. They carried brooms, shovels, mud, and stones with which to clean and ready the runway for landing.

They rode in bullock carts, on bicycles, or simply walked on foot, carrying buckets on their heads and brooms or shovels in their hands. Cars and trucks in the area were requested to help form lines on both sides of the runway. Their tail lights would be used to guide the plane's landing in lieu of the runway lights because there was not enough time to install the new ones.

Just as the flotilla of police and civilian cars and trucks, loaded with equipment and experts, was nearing the airfield, the army of villagers was also beginning to descend there in full force. The stage was set for a showdown against the government's dysfunction, bureaucracy, and lack of planning by that of dynamism, and the spirit of its people.

Faisal took charge of getting the runway ready for landing, while Zoya prepared her team to evacuate passengers quickly and safely upon landing. Irshad took charge of the control tower with a team of engineers and controllers. Their job was to communicate with Akash and install new radars or repair the old ones along with other equipment that would be necessary to land the plane.

The scene inside the plane was that of confusion and fear, as many of the more than 300 passengers onboard were watching live news coverage of their plight on the television monitors embedded in the back of their seats. No one knew for sure what was happening. Some passengers were sympathetic while others were nervous, angry, and demanding answers. Flight attendants had the ridiculously difficult job of keeping anxious passengers calm, but given the potential of a disruptive event, they were trained to avoid any escalation of conflict and to aggressively nip the situation in the bud. Passengers found themselves subjected to strict enforcement of the federal regulations that no person may assault, threaten, intimidate, or interfere with a crew member in the performance of the crew member's duties aboard an aircraft.

"Would you like some tea or coffee?" asked one of the flight attendants to Akash and Priya on the service phone during a temporary lull that prevailed in the cockpit.

"We'll have some coffee, please," replied Akash.

"So what made you become a flight attendant?" asked Akash to Priya while waiting for coffee.

"I got tired of the office job, it was too boring and I found myself too confined. I wanted to travel the world, see places, and meet people.

"Do you still plan to continue after today's incidence?"

"Yes I do."

"You are braver than I am," laughed Akash. "Maybe you should take the pilot's seat."

"No, I think you are doing a great job. I admire your courage to stand up to the Indian bureaucrats. I would have never been able to do what you did today."

"I hope everything works out well. I am taking a huge risk," said Akash nervously, and with a grim face.

"It will. You've got to believe in yourself," replied Priya, as the two sipped on their coffee.

Their conversation was briefly interrupted as the control tower asked Akash to adjust his flight plan towards the new airport, and assured him that everything was being readied as per plan.

"Are you afraid of heights?" asked Irshad shortly thereafter.

"Yes, I am very afraid of heights."

Akash's words reminded Irshad of his own co-pilot, who was also afraid of heights, and how he landed planes by intensely focusing on the runway. The only thing he ever saw was the runway, he used to say. He completely ignored the skyline, especially at night, and anything that reminded him of heights. It was his laser like focus that helped him succeed in his job as a pilot.

Announcements were made through the radio and the speakers from the temple, gurudwara, mosque, and the church to keep the village lights off for the landing. Even the police and emergency vehicles that had surrounded the airport turned their lights off to comply with the request.

Irshad then instructed Akash to make the final announcement before the final descent, and prepare the crew for landing.

The entire plane erupted with cheers and tears of joy as Akash made the final announcement. The mood in the plane turned from gloom to one of jubilance. Many passengers clapped, while others bowed their head and prayed for a safe landing.

"That's my dad," screamed Rohit with pride, with his fists in the air.

Soon, the flight attendants were instructing passengers on how to position themselves for a hard, emergency landing by holding their ankles and head between their knees, in a brace position. Procedures on how to evacuate the plane quickly using the emergency exits and chutes were announced over the speakers.

The entire country came to a standstill, as they prayed for the safety of passengers, while the plans for landing the plane were broadcast on television networks.

"*Mere dost* (My friend), I can't see anything; it's completely dark outside!" shouted Akash nervously on the radio, as the plane descended rapidly towards the airport.

"*Agar dost bola hai, to dost par vishwas rakho, aur iteminan rakho* (If you call me a friend, then put trust in your friend, and have patience). Focus on the steps we discussed," replied Irshad from the control tower, as he watched the plane descend smoothly on the radar.

"Do you believe in angels, Dad?" The words of Shreya and Rohit flashed through his mind, as Akash looked at the family portrait that was sitting in front of him in the cockpit.

"Yes, I do."

"Have you ever seen angels?"

"Yes, I have."

"When? Where?" asked the children with excitement.

"I am looking at two of them right now."

"Dad," said the children shyly, as they hugged and rested their heads on his shoulders.

Irshad was yet another angel sent from heaven, thought Akash, as he prepared for the landing.

Irshad finally sent a text message to his son Faisal, who had been waiting in a sports car on the runway. "Go," said the message, as the plane descended closer to the landing strip. Faisal then called the first car on each side of the runway. Each of them called the car behind them as they started their engines, and turned their lights on. Within seconds, the entire runway was lit on both sides, with Faisal's car in the middle, to guide the plane on the runway. A cacophony of roaring sights and sounds from the engines, head lights, tail lights, and cameras put the nation on edge, as everyone prepared themselves to witness an event of historic proportions that would satisfy the appetite of even the biggest thrill seekers.

As the plane prepared to make its emergency landing on a short runway that was one third the size of a full sized conventional runway, the flight attendants chanted, "Brace, brace, brace," like a mantra.

Irshad then practiced step-by-step landing instructions with Akash -- completing each move: flaps down, slaps down, landing gear down, nose up, and proper landing speed, while still in the air. He made Akash approach the runway several times, just to be sure, because landing accidents accounted for more than a third of all general aviation accidents. The lives of more than 300 passengers were on the line. The first approach for landing was just for practice to build Akash's confidence in the handling of the plane. The second time, Akash came in too high, too fast, and had to abort the landing. The third time, the plane was too low, and too slow, and the plane would have stalled before reaching the landing threshold.

"This is crazy," screamed the home minister, as he watched the events unfold on the television. "They are playing a dangerous game, landing such a huge aircraft with an inexperienced pilot on such a short runway. They are going to get killed. Bring them back to the IGI airport."

"It is too late for that sir," replied the aviation minister. "I don't think they have enough fuel left in the plane. They had to burn excess fuel in the air while circling the airport to minimize the danger of fire upon landing. Besides, they have already refused to follow our plan."

Frustrated home minister murmured something angrily as he paced the room furiously in frustration.

"We are running very low on fuel," screamed Akash, over the radio. "I can hear the engines sputter. The fuel gauge is almost at empty."

"Focus on the landing speed, height, and threshold. You have just enough fuel to land the plane safely. Think of the safety of your family and the passengers. You have to believe in yourself. You can do it," replied Irshad.

Priya quietly pulled out a bookmark from her book and handed it to Akash for inspiration. The bookmark read….

"Answer the Call"

"STOP…Take a moment to turn off the noise coming from the world around you.

Stop and listen…

Listen to the call of your family.

Listen to the call coming from your children.

Listen to the call for friendship coming from people close to you.

Listen to the call of each new day with its brand new possibilities.

Listen to the call of your faith and the one above you calling to lead you to a more positive and happier life.

Go ahead and answer the call."

****

Akash looked at his family portrait, bowed his head in prayer, and rounded the plane with determination, intense mental focus, and exceptional self-control for the fourth attempt. He ruthlessly shed distractions, including his own fear of death. He knew he didn't have enough fuel to miss and go around and try it again. He visualized in his mind where and how he was going to land.

With the passengers still curled into defensive postures and the electricity switched off, Akash readied the plane again for landing. This time, Akash successfully landed the plane on the runway with Irshad's voice guiding him on the radio. The wheels finally hit the tarmac hard, bouncing the plane into the air. The plane hit the ground with enough impact to jerk dentures out of anyone's mouth. Akash pressed the brakes and tightly held the yoke located in the console as if he was holding on to the rope to save his father from falling into the cliff. Images of his father screaming for help flashed in front of him as his knuckles turned white and his arms shook strenuously.

Small airports like the one where they landed, normally host small, single-engine planes, and a few helicopters. But the Boeing 787-300 jet so outsized the small airport that its engines rattled the houses all across the village and its tires left skid marks the length of the runway. Akash had just performed the remarkable feat of landing a huge 330-ton jetliner with the help of an ex-pilot in the control tower. Some called it a miracle, considering the size and condition of the runway. His performance was a work of extraordinary concentration. Tears welled up in Akash's eyes as he rested his head on the back of his seat with a sigh of relief before thanking the crew and passengers for staying calm and helping one another. Passengers in the plane cheered and thanked the crew for a job done brilliantly.

The entire nation erupted with tears and applause as the plane came to a complete stop at the edge of the runway. Jubilant people filled the streets as they danced with pride and shared traditional Indian sweets with one another. The police and emergency vehicles moved in quickly as soon as the plane stopped. The passengers and crew slid out of the plane on inflatable emergency exit chutes and were quickly attended to by a team of nurses and doctors that had converged at the airport under Zoya's leadership.

Looking tired and exhausted with dark circles under his eyes, Akash finally emerged from the cockpit where his family waited with patience, and they gave him a big hug. "We are so proud of you," said his family. Akash then checked the plane twice for any stragglers -- just like his personal hero, Captain Sullenberger of United Airline's flight 1549 that landed on the Hudson River, before exiting with his family.

Accompanied by hundreds of police officers, the deputy police commissioner Mr. Gupta waited outside at the gate, as Akash emerged from the plane with his family. Akash gently kneeled and kissed the tarmac of the land of his parents, the land of his birth, the land he had left more than thirty years ago. Expecting an arrest as ordered by the home minister, Akash then slowly stood up and extended both of his hands out to the deputy police commissioner voluntarily. Instead, the deputy commissioner shook Akash's hand, looked him in the eyes, and thanked him for his courage and leadership. He then escorted the family to the airport's waiting area where Irshad and his team, along with thousands of villagers, gave them a hero's welcome with flowers and garlands. A huge handwritten banner in the front read, "Welcome home," while a befitting song -- Mera Joota Hai Japani, Yeh Patloon Englishtani, Sar Pe Laal Topi Roosi Phir Bhi Dil Hai Hindustani (My shoes are

Japanese/These pants are English/On my head is a red Russian hat/But still, my heart is Hindustani) played on the speakers.

****

16 CIRCLE OF LIFE

The safe but spectacular landing of Flight 126 in the village transformed Akash into a national hero overnight, at a time when people in India and elsewhere were hungry for one. While it was apparent that India was shining economically, it had been losing ground in other areas. There had been rampant exposure of corruption. The rise of hard working billionaires was overshadowed by the rise of *baksheesh billionaires*, (people who got rich by accepting bribes and through corruption). One corruption scandal after another had filled the newspapers. One villager at the landing site summed up the mood in India during an interview, "With so much bad going on, it feels good to have something good going on."

The villagers of Mahan voted to change the name of their village after Akash. Newspapers ran front page stories across India and elsewhere. Fan pages sprang up on the Internet. Akash had a billion Indians promoting him as their hero.

The story of the landing inspired people around the country and millions more around the world, as a perfect example of what was possible with human imagination, determination, and team spirit.

There is a common view amongst Indians that western media unfairly publishes stories about India that only involve cows, poverty, honor killings, call center workers with accents, many-armed gods and goddesses, spiritual traditions, and other exotic, depressing, or weird things. But seeing a happy story of the landing published across the world without any negativity attached to it made every Indian proud.

While the world clamored for Akash's story and people applauded his actions, Akash retained his focus, avoiding the limelight and giving all the credit to Irshad, his family, and the villagers who made it all happen. He remained the husband who made *chai* for his wife in the morning, and a father who put his family's safety and happiness before his own. Within two days after the landing and getting much needed rest from a long and grueling flight, he was hard at work showing his family around the capital, New Delhi, his place of birth. This trip after all, was his wedding anniversary gift to his wife and he wanted it to be a memorable one.

Rohit, a history buff, wanted to see the historic buildings and attend historic events, while Shreya was more interested in shopping for dazzling, colorful, elegant Indian clothing and jewelry. Balancing the children's interests and desires, with those of his childhood friends and other family members turned out to be as difficult of a task for Akash as landing the plane. There was so much to see, experience, and do, in a very short time. Akash often wondered if he really thought he was going to have enough time to see everything on their wish list. From the placid vantage of a laptop, the trip to India looked manageable, but in real time, it was much more challenging.

So, with an air conditioned car, and a driver at their disposal 24/7, each day in Delhi would start with some sight-seeing, followed by shopping, and then dinner with friends and family that would run late into the night.

The family driver, Ramu, short for Ram Singh, was a wiry, 50-something year-old who had been coached by Akash to follow all the road rules and drive safely as the family embarked on a tour of the tri-state area, Delhi, Agra, and Jaipur, popularly known as The Golden Triangle. They had already experienced kamikaze conditions on the roads on a first hand basis. They had seen mangled wrecks of mostly trucks and buses that had collided in a never-ending struggle for possession of narrow, potholed, impossibly overcrowded roads. It became obvious to them in just a few days that many Indians subscribed to the karma school of driving. That meant that it was not crazed driving that killed you, it was an individual's karma, or destiny -- a concept that had the effect of diminishing any sense of personal accountability in drivers.

"Don't worry Sahib," assured Ramu, "everything will be alright. I'll bring you home safely."

And safely he did.

***

"How was it?" "Did you have fun?" "Are you alright?" "I hope it wasn't too hot for you?" "What did you like the most?" "Has India changed a lot since you left?" "How do you like India?" The Kumar family was peppered with such questions as they returned from their trip of the Golden Triangle.

"Everything was beautiful. We all loved it and had lots of fun. While it was true that there was lot of pollution, traffic, dirt, poverty, and all; the sheer beauty of the country, and the love and affection of its people trumped everything," said Akash with a smile, as everyone nodded in agreement.

"What's next on your agenda?"

"First some rest for a few days and some quality time with friends and family, and then on to Ladakh to see the Himalayan Mountains."

"Oh, wow!" "You must be so excited!" "You are so lucky!" "Ladakh is so pretty!" You will love the mountains!" "It's Heaven's Gate!"

And with every well-intentioned exclamation, nervous excitement started to build again as they approached the final leg of their journey in the Himalayan Mountains.

***

The mood was somber as the Kumar family departed from New Delhi to the Leh airport in Ladakh, gazing down more than 30,000 feet. The Jet Airways plane flew across the narrowing triangle of Indian Territory that lay beyond Simla, the old British retreat in the Himalayan foothills north of New Delhi. It was a staging post for travels into what primordial Indians knew as "the land beyond the mountains."

The trip to Ladakh had been arranged by Durga, a two-year-old Indian company that specialized on treks through the Himalayas — a region formerly the exclusive province for trekkers and religious pilgrims willing to trade comfort for the hope of transcendence.

The U.S. State Department does warn Americans to avoid Kashmir, but makes an exception for this tiny Himalayan kingdom. That means that any concerns in Ladakh are far outweighed by the extraordinary surroundings: a scorched desert landscape, the milky-blue Indus River, glassy peaks, and ancient white monasteries. However, the department does warn that it can be difficult to acclimate there without a prescription for Diamox at such high altitudes.

"Julé," greeted Tsewang in traditional Ladakhi language, as the Kumar family emerged from the plane. The young guide with a cheerful disposition drove them through scenic hills toward their hotel.

The first Ladakhi village they came to was a cluster of flat-roofed houses built of mud and straw. It was set in a typical Ladakhi moonscape -- brown and ocher mountainsides bare of vegetation. But the village itself was aflame with color -- the green of ripening crops, the turquoise water and foamy whitecaps of a rushing river, and the reds and yellows worn by Buddhist monks ambling home toward a nearby monastery. In the glow of a setting sun, groups of women and girls were at work harvesting in the fields. Others waved cheerfully from their houses, many of them dressed in the traditional finery visible everywhere in Ladakh -- high felt hats, richly embroidered red shawls, heavy necklaces of silver and turquoise and coral and with long, thick tresses plaited to their waists.

By dusk, the family was comfortably settled in the Shambala Hotel on the outskirts of Leh, a city that seemed more like an overgrown village -- sprawling flat-roofed across an ancient moraine that filled a space between two mountains.

Several of the best-known gompas, or monasteries, were close to Leh, including the Shey and Tikse monasteries that lie within a half-hour's drive south of the city. However, Akash requested a visit to the Spituk monastery, improbably situated above the airport at Leh that he had visited with his father. While Spituk lacked the grandeur of better-known monasteries, with their candle lit libraries of Tibetan scrolls and giant statues of the Buddha, it had an engaging informality. They went there for evening prayers, sitting cross-legged in a pillared hall, while rows of wizened monks intoned their prayers, struck their gongs, and sipped from tiny cups of a yak's-milk tea. A young boy in a maroon robe welcomed everyone as his friends flitted about pouring yak-butter tea into tourists' bowls; he limped toward the back of the windowless monastery's prayer hall, heavy copper pot trailing behind him. He offered a small serving of the creamy broth, a flash of Chiclet-like baby teeth, and that Ladakhi greeting. Then he slipped back into his row and began to sway to the rhythm of the surrounding chants.

The next morning, the family rose before the sun, to a breakfast of fresh yogurt and pomegranate seeds before embarking on their journey in the mountains. They watched as young men took cows out to pasture and women with thick braids and layers of heavy wool cloaks made offerings at a stupa, a religious mound supposedly containing relics of the Buddha.

Shortly after breakfast, the family began their journey, starting in Leh and meandering to Stok and Nimoo — towns separated by death-defying overpasses and landslide-scarred valley walls. At every turn the landscape seemed to change, looking at times like the dunes of Arabia, at others like the pockmarked landscape of Afghanistan or the marigold peaks of Arizona. Never did they glimpse another person, though the offerings of thousands, in the form of white stupas, were sprinkled across the scenery like anthills. In the adjacent valleys they could see the faint purple haze of wild lavender.

Everyone slowly made it to the top of the final hill with the help of walking sticks. The landscape was covered in a thick sea of fog. In the far distance, faded mountains rose in the left, gently leveling off into lowland plains in the east. Beyond there, the pervading fog stretched out indefinitely, eventually commingling with the horizon and becoming indistinguishable from the cloud-filled sky.

Suddenly, Akash murmured something softly as his lips quivered and his body trembled. He was walking in a daze.

"What is it?" asked Aarti.

But he continued walking in a daze slowly toward a rocky precipice without answering.

Aarti signaled everyone to stop following Akash.

"But, Mom," resisted Shreya. "Look where he is going," she repeated, as a faint sense of danger brushed her, like the breath of a cold fog.

"Shush," whispered Aarti.

"He will be alright," she said, as she guided everyone toward a perched ground nearby to sit on.

"No, Mom," pleaded Rohit, as he shook Aarti's arm vigorously. "Don't let him go like this. Stop him. Look where he is going. He will fall off."

"We have taken him as far as we could on this journey. He must cover the rest on his own. It's his personal journey," replied Aarti, with her hands folded under her chin, and tears rolling down her face.

"We will wait for him right here," she continued after a short pause, as they watched Akash from a distance.

Standing alone in a thick mist, barely able to see a few yards ahead, Akash recognized the place as he stood on a ridge. The place looked surreal and quiet beyond description.

Suddenly, once again, Akash was overcome by the images of his father screaming for help over and over, like a movie that he could not turn off. He grabbed his head. Sharp shooting pains of memories flooded Akash's mind sporadically and vigorously, like the monsoons of India. Akash grabbed his head as if to hold the heaviness he felt within. The sweat poured profusely through his pores; as Akash clenched his forehead tighter, his knuckles grew whiter and his mind flooded with flashes that had been haunting him for over thirty years.

Then suddenly, he heard a voice out of nowhere. "Welcome back," said the voice.

"Dad?" wondered Akash, as he turned toward the voice. There he saw a blurry image behind the thick fog. It was hard to see.

"What took you so long?" asked the voice behind the image that became a bit clearer under the soft heavenly light, shining down on him from the sky.

"I was scared," replied Akash, as he tightly hugged his father while sobbing uncontrollably.

"Scared of what?" asked his dad, as they both sat on a boulder.

"I still get nightmares when I think of this place, Dad.

Sometimes, I can't sleep all night. I really tried very hard to save you. I kept pulling on the rope. Look, my hands were even bleeding.

"I know you did. I am thankful to you. But you know something: one has to go when his time comes."

"No Dad, I was not strong enough. I am sorry I could not save you."

"It wasn't your fault. It was my destiny. God wanted me back."

"I miss you Dad."

"I miss you too beta. I have been waiting for you for a very long time. I knew you would come back to see me someday.

"I wanted to, but I was too afraid to come here."

"So tell me, how is life in America? How is Parvati?"

"Everything is fine Dad. Jhai ji also came to see you with us," said Akash with excitement.

"Where did they go? They were right here with me a few minutes ago," wondered Akash as he looked around.

"Who else came with you?"

"My wife, Aarti, and our children, Shreya and Rohit; they also came to see you. They must have stepped away somewhere. I am sure they will be here in a few minutes," continued Akash with nervous excitement.

"Tell me more about everyone! How old are the children? What do you do? What does Aarti do?"

"I am a professor at a university. Aarti is a doctor, and both children are in school," said Akash proudly. "They all miss you very much."

"I wish I could be with you also. I miss spending time

with you and Parvati. I miss not being able to play with you."

Suddenly, Akash's dad became quiet and went into deep thoughts.

"What happened? What are you thinking?"

"You know something," he replied after a brief pause. "I was blessed to have received a good education in India, become a doctor and go to America. I was blessed to have a wonderful wife like Parvati and a beautiful son like you. I left India because I wanted to give you a good education and our family a good life. But my dream was to come back once you were grown up so that I could do something meaningful and make a difference in the lives of our people. Most of India lived in villages with just a few doctors, combined. Most doctors wanted to go abroad or work in the big cities where there was money. The government alone couldn't meet all the healthcare needs of everyone because of the large population, inadequate infrastructure, and illiteracy. My dream was to bridge that gap by reaching to everyone."

"How would you have reached everyone?"

"Akash se," (through the sky).

"Akash se?" asked Akash with a puzzled look.

"You see, if Lord Indra can send the rains through the sky to every corner of the world, then why can't we shower education and healthcare through the sky?"

"My dream was to connect all villages through a satellite, and provide education and healthcare to all villages across India."

"The problem is not just a lack of healthcare, but also a lack of education. The vast majority of sickness in villages could be prevented with clean water, waste-disposal systems, and learning about simple things like hand-washing, nutrition, breast-feeding, and other home remedies. They need to end deadly superstitions about health, discrimination against women and Untouchables. You need a doctor and a teacher to accomplish that."

There was complete silence for a minute as Akash waited anxiously for his father to finish the story.

"I know I have given you nothing but grief in life. I left you at such a young age when you needed a father. Your mother had to raise you by herself. I know I have no right to ask you for anything," continued his dad, after a short pause. "But can I ask for one last favor? Please!"

"Please don't say that. You were the best dad anyone could have asked for. You have the right to ask for anything you want. I am your son," pleaded Akash.

"Will you fulfill my dream? Will you sacrifice comfort for service and luxury for joy? Will you do something so beautiful? Will you come back home?"

"Yes, yes, yes. Yes, I will," promised Akash, as he cried on his father's shoulders.

"Thank you so much," said his dad as the two hugged each other in the peace and quiet of the early morning sun that was shining brilliantly in a clear blue sky, as the fog and dew started to dissipate.

***

"Dad," murmured Akash, as he looked around for his dad on the boulder where he had fallen asleep.

"Dad!" screamed Akash hysterically. "Where did you go?" He looked everywhere but could not find him.

Suddenly, once again, Akash was overcome by the images of his father screaming for help over and over, like a movie that he could not turn off.

"Dad," screamed Akash at the top of his lungs as he grabbed his head in pain and kneeled on the ground.

"Close your eyes and change your nightmare into a

dream," the voice of Dr. Joshi echoed in the mountains from the sky. "A dream you truly wished had happened instead of the nightmare."

"I can't," screamed Akash in pain. His father kept screaming for help.

"Do it until memories of the nightmare are tamed, and the new dream takes its place," said the voice as it became louder and louder.

"You can do it."

Slowly, Akash gathered himself, and started to pull the rope that was slipping through his hands. He used the boulder to support his body, and pulled the rope with all his might.

A few minutes later, he saw his father climb back up as he lay exhausted, and in pain by the boulder with his hands bleeding from the cuts and his body from the bruises.

His father came over, kneeled, kissed his forehead, and started to clean him up before providing first-aid. He gave him some water and gently ran his fingers through his hair with affection and gratitude.

A few minutes passed, and then his father said "Let's go before it gets too dark. Your mom is waiting for us."

***

In the end, what we pay the most attention to defines us. How you choose to spend the irreplaceable hours of your life literally transforms you.

So, write your dreams, not your nightmares.

****

GLOSSARY

GLOSSARY OF HINDI WORDS USED IN ITALICS AND THEIR MEANING AS PROVIDED IN WIKIPEDIA.

Chapter 01

A **sari** or **saree** is a strip of unstitched cloth, worn by women, ranging from four to nine yards in length that is draped over the body in various styles which is native to the Indian Subcontinent.

Deepavali or **Diwali,** popularly known as the **"festival of lights,"** is a five-day Hindu festival[3] which starts on Dhanteras, celebrated on the thirteenth lunar day of Krishna paksha (dark fortnight) of the Hindu calendar month Ashwin and ends on Bhaubeej, celebrated on second lunar day of Shukla paksha (bright fortnight) of the Hindu calendar month Kartik. Dhanteras usually falls eighteen days after Dussehra. In the Gregorian calendar, Diwali falls between mid-October and mid-November.

Diwali is an official holiday in India,[5] Nepal, Sri Lanka, Myanmar, Mauritius, Guyana, Trinidad & Tobago, Suriname, Malaysia, Singapore and Fiji.

For Hindus, Diwali is one of the most important festivals of the year and is celebrated in families by performing traditional activities together in their homes.

A **mantra** is a sound, syllable, word, or group of words that is considered capable of creating transformation. Its use and type varies according to the school and philosophy associated with the mantra.

A **Diya, divaa, deepa, deepam,** or **deepak** is an oil lamp usually made from clay, with a cotton wick dipped in ghee or vegetable oils. Clay diyas are often used temporarily as lighting for special occasions, while diyas made of brass are permanent fixtures in homes and temples. Diyas are native to India, and are often used in Hindu, Sikh, Jain and Zoroastrian religious festivals such as Diwali or the Kushti ceremony.

A **kurta** is a traditional item of clothing worn in Afghanistan, Pakistan, Nepal, India, Bangladesh, and Sri Lanka. It is a loose shirt falling either just above or somewhere below the knees of the wearer, and is worn by men.

Lehenga choli, is the traditional clothing of women in Rajasthan, Gujarat, Madhya Pradesh, Uttar Pradesh, Bihar, Haryana, Himachal Pradesh and Uttarakhand in India.

Kālī, also known as **Kālikā**, is the Hindu goddess associated with empowerment, shakti. The name Kali comes from *kāla*, which means black, time, death, lord of death, Shiva. Since Shiva is called Kāla—the eternal time—Kālī, his consort, also means "Time" or "Death" (as in time has come). Hence, Kāli is the Goddess of Time and Change. Although sometimes presented as dark and violent, her earliest incarnation as a figure of annihilator of evil forces still has some influence. Various Shakta Hindu cosmologies, as well as Shākta Tantric beliefs, worship her as the ultimate reality or *Brahman*. She is also revered as **Bhavatārini** (literally "redeemer of the universe"). Comparatively recent devotional movements largely conceive Kāli as a benevolent mother goddess.

Rama is the seventh avatar of the god Vishnu in Hinduism,[1] and a king of Ayodhya in Hindu scriptures. In a few Rama-centric sects, Rama is considered the Supreme Being, rather than an avatar. Rama was born in Suryavansha (Ikshvaku Vansham) later known as Raghuvansha after king Raghu.

Rāvaṇa, (also known by other names) is the primary antagonist character of the Hindu epic Ramayana; who was the Rakshasa (demon worshiping) king of Sri Lanka (Heladiva). In the classic text, he is mainly depicted negatively, kidnapping Rama's wife Sita, to claim vengeance on Rama and his brother Lakshmana for having cut off the nose of his sister Surpanakha ,who got attracted and was forcing God Rama to marry her in spite of Him being married to Goddess Sita.

Chapter 02

Vishnu is a Vedic Supreme God (including his different avatars) in Hinduism, and is venerated as the Supreme Being in Vaishnavism. Lord Vishnu is the all-pervading essence of all beings, the master of—and beyond—the past, present and future, the creator and destroyer of all existences, one who supports, sustains and governs the universe and originates and develops all elements within.

Sheshnag, is the divine serpent in Indian mythology.

A **Bhajan** is any type of devotional song. It has no fixed form: it may be as simple as a mantra or kirtan or as sophisticated as the dhrupad or kriti with music based on classical ragas and talas. It is normally lyrical, expressing love for the Divine. The name, a cognate of bhakti, meaning religious devotion, suggests its importance to the bhakti movement that spread from the south of India throughout the entire subcontinent in the Moghul era.

Beta – Son but often used for a daughter also.

Chapter 03

Aloo gobi, also spelled **alu gobi**, **aloo gobhi** or **alu gawbi**, is a dry Indian, Nepali and Pakistani cuisine dish made with potatoes (*aloo*), cauliflower (*gob(h)i*) and Indian spices. It is yellowish in color, due to the use of turmeric, and occasionally contains kalonji and curry leaves. Other common ingredients include garlic, ginger, onion, coriander stalks, tomato, peas, and cumin. A number of variations and similar dishes exist, but the name remains the same.

Mattar paneer is a north Indian dish consisting of paneer and peas in a slightly sweet and spicy sauce. Mattar paneer masala is probably the most popular curry found in all over India.[1] First, the cottage cheese is prepared in the traditional method. The base is prepared with cumin seeds, garam masala, vine ripened tomatoes and the green peas and paneer cheese cubes are added for stir frying on high heat.

Chutney (also called **chatney**) is an Indian word meaning sauce. It refers to a wide-ranging family of condiments from Indian cuisine/Pakistani cuisine that usually contain some mixture of spice(s), vegetable(s) and/or fruit(s). There are many varieties of chutney.

Chutneys may be either wet or dry, and can have a coarse to a fine texture. The Indian word refers to fresh and pickled preparations indiscriminately, with preserves often sweetened. Several Indian languages use the word for fresh preparations only.

Kheer is a rice pudding, which is a traditional South Asian sweet dish. It is made by boiling rice or broken wheat with milk and sugar, and flavoured with cardamom, raisins, saffron, cashew nuts, pistachios or almonds. It is typically served during a meal or also consumed alone as a dessert.

Ghanti, bells are an integral part of puja (worship) in Hinduism. They are used while performing Aarti. The bell sounds help to drown any inauspicious or disturbing noises.

Dhoop - India has a rich tradition of incense making that goes back millennia. Many Indian incenses have a unique scent that is not found in any other part of the globe. Incense sticks formed around bamboo are known as agarbatti or agarbathi, while other main forms of incense are cones and logs or dhoops, which are incense paste formed into pyramid shapes or log shapes, and then dried.

The **Gāyatrī Mantra** is a highly revered mantra, based on a Vedic Sanskrit verse from a hymn of the Rigveda, attributed to the rishi (sage) Viśvāmitra. The mantra is named for its vedic gāyatrī metre. As the verse can be interpreted to invoke the deva

Savitr, it is often called **Sāvitrī** Its recitation is traditionally preceded by *oṃ* and the formula *bhūr bhuvaḥ svaḥ*, known as the *mahāvyāhṛti* ("great utterance").

Pūjā or alternative transliteration **Pooja**, is a religious ritual performed by Hindus as an offering to various deities, distinguished persons, or special guests. This is also been followed by Buddhists and Sikhs to honour various beliefs. In Hinduism, it is done on a variety of occasions and settings, from daily *puja* done in the home, to temple ceremonies and large festivals, or to begin a new venture.

Chana masala, also known as **chole masala** or **channay** (plural) is a popular Punjabi dish in Pakistani and Indian cuisine. The main ingredient is chickpeas (called "chana" in Hindustani). It is fairly dry and spicy with a sour citrus note.

Chapati, Chapatti, or **Chapathi** is an unleavened flatbread (also known as *roti*) from India. It is a common staple of cuisine in South Asia as well as amongst South Asian expatriates throughout the world. Chapatis are one of the most common forms in which wheat, the staple of northern South Asia, is consumed. Chapati is a form of *roti* or *rotta* (bread). The words are often used interchangeably. While *roti* or *rotta* refers to any flat unleavened bread, chapati is a roti made of whole wheat flour and cooked on a *tava* (flat skillet).

Chapter 04

Hindi – National language of India

Didi – Older sister

Thali – Tray

Ganesha, also spelled **Ganesa** and **Ganesh**, also known as **Pillaiyar, Ganapati** and **Vinayaka**, is one of the best-known and most widely worshipped deities in the Hindu pantheon. His image is found throughout India and Nepal. Hindu sects worship him regardless of affiliations. Devotion to Ganesha is widely diffused and extends to Jains, Buddhists, and beyond India.

Chapter 05

In the Hindu epic Mahābhārata, the **Pandava** are the five acknowledged sons of Pandu, by his two wives Kunti and Madri. Their names are Yudhisthira, Bhima, Arjuna, Nakula and Sahadeva. All five brothers were married to the same woman, Draupadi. (Each brother also had multiple other wives.

Together, the brothers fought and prevailed in a great war against their cousins the Kauravas, which came to be known as the Battle of Kurukshetra.

Arjun is a first name of a male, based on Arjuna, a legendary hero who is considered as the greatest archer ever and a central character in the Hindu epic Mahabharata.

The term **Kaurava** is a Sanskrit term, that means the descendants of Kuru, a legendary king who is the ancestor of many of the characters of the Mahābhārata.

In the Hindu epic the Mahābhārata, **Duryodhana**, 'difficult to fight with', his real name was Suyodhana) is the eldest son of the blind king Dhritarashtra by Queen Gandhari, the eldest of the one hundred Kaurava brothers. Emperor of the world (which then meant Emperor of India, or Bharatvarsha as it was then known), he was the cousin and the chief antagonist of the Pandavas.

Krishna, is the eighth avatar of the Vedic Supreme God Vishnu in Hinduism. The word Krishna means *one with dark complexion* and *one who attracts all.* The name Krishna appears as the 57th and 550th name of Lord Vishnu in Vishnu Sahasranama of Mahabharata. The name Krishna is also amongst the 24 Keshava Namas of Lord Vishnu which are recited and praised at the beginning of all Vedic pujas in Hinduism.

Dharma is the Law that "upholds, supports or maintains the regulatory order of the universe", Dharma has the Sanskrit root dhri, which means "that without which nothing can stand" or "that which maintains the stability and harmony of the universe."

Hinduism, Jainism, Buddhism, and Sikhism all have the idea of *dharma* at their core, where it points to the purification and moral transformation of human beings. Dharma is not the same as Religion. Though differing in some particulars, all concur that the goal of human life is moksha or nirvana, in which the ultimate nature of *dharma* (as cosmic law) is apprehended experientially.

Chapter 09

Baoji, is a term used in north India for father.

Sari - A sari is traditional Indian dress that dates back to the Indus Valley Civilization as far back as 2800-1800 BC. Hindu culture believes that any cloth pierced by a needle was impure, so saris were woven of pure cotton. Over time, silk and other threads were woven together on hand looms to make intricate designs and patterns.

White is considered pure and is worn during rituals and for **mourning**.

Plain white sari is traditionally worn by a widow.

A **bindi** is a forehead decoration worn in South Asia (particularly India, Bangladesh, Nepal, Sri Lanka and Mauritius) and Southeast Asia. Traditionally it is a bright dot of red color applied in the center of the forehead close to the eyebrows, but it can also consist of a sign or piece of jewelry worn at this location.

In addition to the bindi, in India, a vermilion mark in the parting of the hair just above the forehead is worn by married women as commitment to long-life and well-being of their husbands.

During all Hindu marriage ceremonies, the groom applies sindoor on the parting in the bride's hair. The bride must wipe off her red bindi once she becomes a widow. This can be seen as symbolic and shows her status in society. Widows can continue to wear the black bindi but with a white sari.

Sindoor is a traditional red or orange-red colored cosmetic powder from India, usually worn by married women along the parting of their hair. Usage of sindoor denotes that a woman is married in many Hindu communities, and ceasing to wear it usually implies widowhood. The main component of traditional sindoor is usually vermilion.

Chapter 11

Yogais a commonly known generic term for the physical, mental, and spiritual practices or disciplines which originated in ancient India with a view to attain a state of permanent peace. Yoga has also been popularly defined as "union with the divine" in other contexts and traditions.

Yoga nidra or "yogi sleep" is a sleep-like state which yogis report to experience during their meditations.

Samādhi in Hinduism, Buddhism, Jainism, Sikhism and yogic schools is a higher level of concentrated meditation, or *dhyāna*. It has been described as a non-dualistic state of consciousness in which the consciousness of the experiencing subject becomes one with the experienced object, and in which the mind becomes still, one-pointed or concentrated while the person remains conscious.

Chapter 13

Shahrukh Khan, informally referred as **SRK**, is an Indian film actor. Referred to in the media as "Badshah of Bollywood", "King Khan", "King of Romance" and "The King of Bollywood", Khan has acted in 75 Hindi films in genres ranging from romantic dramas to action thrillers. His contributions to the film industry have garnered him numerous achievements, including fourteen Filmfare Awards from thirty nominations. His eighth Filmfare Best Actor Award win made him the most awarded Bollywood actor of all time in that category, tied only with actor Dilip Kumar. In 2005, the Government of India honoured him with the Padma Shri for his contributions towards Indian cinema.

Bollywood is the informal term popularly used for the Hindi-language film industry based in Mumbai (Bombay), Maharashtra, India. The term is often incorrectly used to refer to the whole of Indian cinema; however, it is only a part of the total Indian film industry, which includes other production centres producing films in multiple languages. Bollywood is the largest film producer in India and one of the largest centres of film production in the world.

Prasād is a material substance of food that is a religious offering in both Hinduism and Sikhism, which is consumed by worshippers.

Chapter 14

A **g`ajra** is a flower garland which women in Pakistan, India and Bangladesh wear during traditional festivals. It is made usually of jasmine; in South India, crossandra and barleria are also widely used in gajras. It can be worn both on the bun and with the braid coiling. Women usually wear these when they wear sarees.

The gajra is an ornament that is purely meant to decorate a hairstyle and does not generally aid in holding a bun in place.

Namaste, Namaskar/Namaskaram, is a common spoken valediction or salutation originating from the Hindus and Buddhists in the Indian Subcontinent and also in Japan. It is a customary greeting when individuals meet, and a valediction upon their parting. A non-contact form of salutation is traditionally preferred in India and Nepal; Namaste is the most common form of such a salutation.

When spoken to another person, it is commonly accompanied by a slight bow made with hands pressed together, palms touching and fingers pointed upwards, in front of the chest. This gesture, can also be performed wordlessly and carries the same meaning.

Swagat – Welcome

Kanyādān ("gift of a virgin or "gift of a maiden") is the most highly valued Hindu wedding ritual. There are different interpretations regarding kanyādān across South Asia. Kanyadaan is a ritual in which the bride's father entrusts her daughter to the groom, who is at the time of marriage considered to be a form of Lord Vishnu.)

Chapter 15

Pratigya – a vow or a pledge

A **Gurdwara**, meaning *the Gateway to the Guru*, is the place of worship for Sikhs however people of all faiths are welcomed in the Gurdwara.

SOURCES

Special thanks to the following sources that were used to complete this novel.

INSPIRATION

Japneet Singh's Father Hopes to Prevent Future Accidents ... (n.d.). Retrieved from http://india.blogs.nytimes.com/2012/10/03/japneet-singhs-father-hopes-to-prevent -future-accidents/

India's schoolchildren face deadly roadways - Hawaii News ... (n.d.). Retrieved from http://www.staradvertiser.com/news/20121003_Indias_schoolc hildren_face_deadly_ro adways.html?id=172455191

Chapter 01

Appleford - Appleford. (n.d.). Retrieved from http://www.applefordestate.com/

Musings of an Unknown Indian: Wish you all a very Happy ... (n.d.). Retrieved from http://notapennyformythoughts.blogspot.com/2009/10/wish-you-all-very-happy.html

How to celebrate Diwali in IndiaBreathedreamgo. (n.d.). Retrieved from http://breathedreamgo.com/2011/10/how-to-celebrate-diwali-in-india/

Puja Vidhi. (n.d.). Retrieved from http://pujavidhi.blogspot.com/

Satymeva Jayate. (n.d.). Retrieved from http://miliriri.blogspot.com/

The Story of Diwali. (n.d.). Retrieved from
http://members.tripod.com/~jennifer_polan/diwali.html

It's A Love Story. (n.d.). Retrieved from
http://chellisandalex.blogspot.com/

NOVA | One Night in an E.R. - PBS: Public Broadcasting
Service. (n.d.). Retrieved from
http://www.pbs.org/wgbh/nova/body/one-night-emergency-
room.html

Chapter 02

Lake Leelanau Vacation Rental - VRBO 66137 - 2 BR Lake ...
(n.d.). Retrieved from http://www.vrbo.com/66137

villas at island club - Kissimmee Forum - TripAdvisor. (n.d.).
Retrieved from http://www.tripadvisor.com/ShowTopic-
g34352-i79-k2144991-Villas_at_island_club-K
issimmee_Florida.html

U of I Admissions: Blog » Elise. (n.d.). Retrieved from
http://blog.admissions.illinois.edu/?author=66

Missing the point: The real stakes in the smartphone wars. (n.d.).
Retrieved from http://esr.ibiblio.org/?p=2061

Blue Devils Battery Book - YouTube. (n.d.). Retrieved from
http://www.youtube.com/watch?v=3QnMAvI4yLk

BARNES & NOBLE | Hell's Corner (Camel Club Series #5) by
... (n.d.). Retrieved from
http://www.barnesandnoble.com/w/hells-corner-david-
baldacci/1023905787

Eating Clean for 30 days Challenge [Archive] - John Stone ...
(n.d.). Retrieved from
http://forums.johnstonefitness.com/archive/index.php/t-
20872.html

I feel thirsty all the day whatever the amount of water I ... (n.d.).
Retrieved from
http://answers.yahoo.com/question/index?qid=2007071605570
2AAo3zKI

www.asstr.org. (n.d.). Retrieved from
http://www.asstr.org/files/Authors/Amanda_Serve/Family%2
0Feud%20III/27%20Family%
20Feud%20III.html

The 7 Habits of Highly Effective People: Stephen R. Covey ...
(n.d.). Retrieved from http://www.amazon.com/The-Habits-
Highly-Effective-People/dp/product-description/
0671708635

Important quotes from Covey's 7 habits. (n.d.). Retrieved from
http://faculty.weber.edu/molpin/healthclasses/1110/coveystuff
.htm

Personal Due Diligence | What works has changed. (n.d.).
Retrieved from http://personalduediligence.com/

Chapter - 03

Island Politics · Oak Harbor Changes City Ordinances to ...
(n.d.). Retrieved from http://www.islandpolitics.org/?p=8971

Prospect Park Advocate. (n.d.). Retrieved from
http://brooklynparks.blogspot.com/

How would you describe a sunset to a blind man? - Yahoo!
Answers. (n.d.). Retrieved from
http://answers.yahoo.com/question/index?qid=1006022209626

No letters, but received direct deposit or check in mail ... (n.d.).
Retrieved from
http://answers.yahoo.com/question/index?qid=2008051609394
8AA00NUe

First Dually Experience, Chevy 3500 HD in Carrier Towing Forum. (n.d.). Retrieved from http://tow411.yuku.com/topic/108814/First-Dually-Experience-Chevy-3500-HD

Irony - Definition and More from the Free Merriam-Webster ... (n.d.). Retrieved from http://www.merriam-webster.com/dictionary/irony

Are you alone righT now? - Yahoo! Answers. (n.d.). Retrieved from http://answers.yahoo.com/question/index?qid=20070904151053AAWOfNa

No Internet - YouTube. (n.d.). Retrieved from http://www.youtube.com/watch?v=eedJUqlqj3M

Countryfolk Keepsakes. (n.d.). Retrieved from http://countryfolkkeepsakes.blogspot.com/

Poem: A Military Son's Life - Scrapbook.com: Scrapbooking ... (n.d.). Retrieved from http://www.scrapbook.com/poems/doc/46179/27.html

Prayer in Hinduism - Wikipedia, the free encyclopedia. (n.d.). Retrieved from http://en.wikipedia.org/wiki/Prayer_in_Hinduism

A Moment of Zen: Early Morning Sunrays. (n.d.). Retrieved from http://jeffreystedfast.blogspot.com/2010/06/early-morning-sunrays.html

Chiropractor Greenville, SC New Patient Special Free Spinal Exam. (n.d.). Retrieved from http://www.chiropractor-greenville.com/

ROFESSIONAL ESPONSIBILITY OCIAL ONTRACT WITH UMANITY. (n.d.). Retrieved from http://www.ama-assn.org/resources/doc/ethics/decofprofessional.pdf

Hurricane Sandy BEGINS - 10/29/12 - YouTube. (n.d.).
Retrieved from
http://www.youtube.com/watch?v=vE0N2KRELcc

Does everything really happen for a reason? - Yahoo! Answers.
(n.d.). Retrieved from
http://answers.yahoo.com/question/index?qid=2012043016594
6AAQXdGP

Old School Walleye Fishing Family Secrets. (n.d.). Retrieved
from http://www.oldschoolwalleyefishing.com/

"The outcast works up the nerve to talk to the popular kid ...
(n.d.). Retrieved from
http://www.collegehumor.com/article/5383940/the-outcast-
works-up-the-nerve-to-ta
lk-to-the-popular-kid

Why do I still love him? When will I be happy? What is wrong ...
(n.d.). Retrieved from
http://answers.yahoo.com/question/index?qid=2008110613001
1AAT6rVC

True Woman | Female Beauty Matters. (n.d.). Retrieved from
http://www.truewoman.com/?id=1718

MENTALLY-ILL ROADSIDE DESTITUTE,PSYCHIATRIC
CARE, PSYCHIATRIC ... (n.d.). Retrieved from
http://shraddharehabilitationfoundation.org/mental-health.htm

Psychiatric Demands Jump as India Battles Mental Illness ...
(n.d.). Retrieved from
http://www.pbs.org/newshour/bb/health/july-dec09/india_12-
29.html

Journeys of Ms. Two Spoiled Kitties. (n.d.). Retrieved from
http://mstwospoiledkitties.blogspot.com/

BARNES & NOBLE | Before I Fall by Lauren Oliver |
NOOK Book ... (n.d.). Retrieved from
http://www.barnesandnoble.com/w/before-i-fall-lauren-
oliver/1100151137

Chapter - 04

Changing Places. (n.d.). Retrieved from
http://www.woodka.com/

Sweet Home Utah! (n.d.). Retrieved from
http://rolltideennisfamily.blogspot.com/

Seven Deadly Sins as per Mahatma Gandhi - WELCOME TO
MAHATMA ... (n.d.). Retrieved from
http://www.mkgandhi.org/mgmnt.htm

NFP and Me. (n.d.). Retrieved from
http://nfpandme.blogspot.com/

ROFESSIONAL ESPONSIBILITY OCIAL ONTRACT
WITH UMANITY. (n.d.). Retrieved from http://www.ama-
assn.org/resources/doc/ethics/decofprofessional.pdf

Rotherham Harriers and Athletics Club (RHAC)Trail Running ...
(n.d.). Retrieved from
http://www.hmarston.pwp.blueyonder.co.uk/rhac/index.htm

Mahatma Gandhi Quotes - Squidoo : Welcome to Squidoo.
(n.d.). Retrieved from http://www.squidoo.com/mahatma-
gandhi-quotes

Lasting ties of love - Indian Link, Linking Indians in ... (n.d.).
Retrieved from http://www.indianlink.com.au/features/lasting-
ties-of-love/

Diary of a High-Functioning Person with Schizophrenia ... (n.d.).
Retrieved from

http://www.scientificamerican.com/article.cfm?id=diary-of-a-high-function

The 30 Best Inspiring Anecdotes of All Times. (n.d.). Retrieved from http://www.liraz.com/Anecdote.htm

Michael Libbe Photography - Musings about photography ... (n.d.). Retrieved from http://blog.michaellibbephotography.com/

Amanda Goes to Church. (n.d.). Retrieved from http://amandagoestochurch.blogspot.com/

Crooked Tiara. (n.d.). Retrieved from http://www.crookedtiara.com/

I did it... my first injection! - Hepatitis Message Board ... (n.d.). Retrieved from http://www.healthboards.com/boards/hepatitis/661529-i-did-my-first-injection.htm
l

"How's Your Love life?". (n.d.). Retrieved from http://hylovelife.blogspot.com/

Chapter 05

Sweet Home Utah! (n.d.). Retrieved from http://rolltideennisfamily.blogspot.com/

Seven Deadly Sins as per Mahatma Gandhi - WELCOME TO MAHATMA ... (n.d.). Retrieved from http://www.mkgandhi.org/mgmnt.htm

Kurukshetra War - Wikipedia, the free encyclopedia. (n.d.). Retrieved from http://en.wikipedia.org/wiki/Kurukshetra_war

A Summary of the Bhagavadgita - Hindu Website, Hinduism ... (n.d.). Retrieved from http://www.hinduwebsite.com/summary.asp

How can i help my friend find god? - Yahoo! Answers. (n.d.). Retrieved from http://answers.yahoo.com/question/index?qid=2006080722121 5AASFyLO

New Song Underground. (n.d.). Retrieved from http://newsongunderground.blogspot.com/

Partnership for Johnson Valley. (n.d.). Retrieved from http://pfjv.org/

Front wheel drive towing and launching / 223361. (n.d.). Retrieved from http://forums.iboats.com/trailers-towing/front-wheel-drive-towing-launching-2233 61.html

Are You Ready To Create A Life Beyond Imagination? (n.d.). Retrieved from http://www.revolutioniz.com/

Word Obsession. (n.d.). Retrieved from http://writersprite.livejournal.com/

Articles : Multicultural Center. (n.d.). Retrieved from http://multiculturalcenter.osu.edu/articles/the-americanization-of-mental-illnes s/

Articles : Multicultural Center. (n.d.). Retrieved from http://multiculturalcenter.osu.edu/articles/the-americanization-of-mental-illnes s/

Reidbord's Reflections - Part 2. (n.d.). Retrieved from http://blog.stevenreidbordmd.com/?paged=2

Cancer Care Quality Measures - St. Mary Medical Center ...
(n.d.). Retrieved from
http://www.stmaryhealthcare.org/body.cfm?id=556697

Shimojo Masao (6): The countries of the Confucian cultural ...
(n.d.). Retrieved from
http://ampontan.wordpress.com/2009/12/08/shimojo-masao-
6-the-countries-of-the-co
nfucian-cultural-sphere/

Has Psychiatry Really Abandoned Psychotherapy? Behind the
New ... (n.d.). Retrieved from
http://psychcentral.com/blog/archives/2011/04/03/has-
psychiatry-really-abandoned
-psychotherapy-the-story-behind-the-new-york-times-story/

Chapter 06

Teaching, No Greater Call. (n.d.). Retrieved from
http://www.lds.org/gospellibrary/materials/teachingnogreater/
Start%20Here.pdf

Dual Diagnoses Treatment | Dual Diagnoses Therapy ... (n.d.).
Retrieved from
http://www.southcoastrecovery.com/dual_diagnoses_treatment.
html

Welcome to Michigan Integrative Psychiatry, PC! (n.d.).
Retrieved from
http://michiganintegrative.com/MIP%20Welcome%20letter.pdf

San Jose Dentist - Rose Park Dental - Dr. Tina Nguyen - Home.
(n.d.). Retrieved from
http://www.roseparkdental.net/home.htm

Welcome to Michigan Integrative Psychiatry, PC! (n.d.).
Retrieved from
http://michiganintegrative.com/MIP%20Welcome%20letter.pdf

New Albany Health Associates. (n.d.). Retrieved from
http://www.nahealthassoc.com/

Brats Blog of Shadows. (n.d.). Retrieved from
http://bratsblogofshadows.blogspot.com/

Understanding mental health problems - Mind. (n.d.). Retrieved
from http://www.mind.org.uk/mental_health_a-
z/8034_understanding_mental_health_proble
ms

MidKnight Inventors » "You never forget your FIRST
Robotics!". (n.d.). Retrieved from http://firstrobotics1923.org/

Karen | Problem Gambling. (n.d.). Retrieved from
http://www.problemgambling.vic.gov.au/main/story/karen-0

PsychiatryOnline | Psychiatric News | News Article. (n.d.).
Retrieved from
http://psychiatryonline.org/article.aspx?articleid=109820

Welcome to the Road. (n.d.). Retrieved from http://welcome-to-
the-road.blogspot.com/

Page 5 - Christmas Blessings - Romance - Literotica.com. (n.d.).
Retrieved from http://www.literotica.com/s/christmas-
blessings?page=5

Karuna Counseling's Newsletter Articles | Karuna therapists ...
(n.d.). Retrieved from http://karunacounseling.wordpress.com/

Real • Creative • Fun - Home. (n.d.). Retrieved from
http://www.jonescustomphoto.net/

Chapter 07

French Women for All Seasons; A Year of Secrets, Recipes ...
(n.d.). Retrieved from
http://www.scribd.com/doc/91433310/French-Women-for-

All-Seasons-A-Year-of-Secret
s-Recipes-Pleasure

Media — Walk and Talk outdoor psychotherapy. (n.d.).
Retrieved from http://www.walkandtalk.com/media.html

Shrunken Heads and Enlarged Egos. (n.d.). Retrieved from
http://christophertmurray.blogspot.com/

Custom boat covers - Winter Boat Covers - Fisher Canvas ...
(n.d.). Retrieved from http://www.fishercanvas.com/

Health | Cervantes. (n.d.). Retrieved from
http://abluteau.wordpress.com/category/health/

When does psychotherapy work? | TIME.com - Health &
Family ... (n.d.). Retrieved from
http://healthland.time.com/2010/08/09/when-does-
psychotherapy-work/

BreathSpace. (n.d.). Retrieved from
http://breathspace.blogspot.com/

post traumatic stress disorder - iftikhar ul haq. (n.d.). Retrieved
from
http://ulhaqcom.wetpaint.com/page/post+traumatic+stress+di
sorder

Post-traumatic stress disorder (PTSD) - MayoClinic.com. (n.d.).
Retrieved from http://www.mayoclinic.com/health/post-
traumatic-stress-disorder/DS00246

PTSD: Brain Scans May Help Diagnosis in Army Veterans -
TIME. (n.d.). Retrieved from
http://www.time.com/time/nation/article/0,8599,1956315,00.h
tml

Post-traumatic stress disorder (PTSD) - MayoClinic.com. (n.d.).
Retrieved from http://www.mayoclinic.com/health/post-

traumatic-stress-disorder/DS00246/METHOD=p
rint

PTSD Disorder | PTSD Diagnosis - Hospital Soup - Hospital ...
(n.d.). Retrieved from http://www.hospitalsoup.com/hc/ptsd-
disorder-ptsd-diagnosis/

Brain-imaging tool may offer quick mental-health diagnostics.
(n.d.). Retrieved from
http://www.research.va.gov/news/research_highlights/brain-
102007.cfm

Helping Heroes: Brain Scans For PTSD - NewsChannel5.com ...
(n.d.). Retrieved from
http://www.newschannel5.com/story/16536470/helping-
heroes-brain-scans-for-ptsd

Brain Scans for PTSD -- In Depth Doctor's Interview | Medical
... (n.d.). Retrieved from
http://www.ivanhoe.com/channels/p_channelstory.cfm?storyid
=28619

Helping Heroes: Brain Scans For PTSD - NewsChannel5.com ...
(n.d.). Retrieved from
http://www.newschannel5.com/story/16536470/helping-
heroes-brain-scans-for-ptsd

BARNES & NOBLE | The Devil You Know (Morgan Kingsley
Series ... (n.d.). Retrieved from
http://www.barnesandnoble.com/w/devil-you-know-jenna-
black/1100297729?ean=978055
3590456

PTSD: Brain Scans May Help Diagnosis in Army Veterans -
TIME. (n.d.). Retrieved from
http://www.time.com/time/nation/article/0,8599,1956315,00.h
tml

Gamasutra - Features - Cognitive Flow: The Psychology of ... (n.d.). Retrieved from http://gamasutra.com/view/feature/166972/cognitive_flow_th e_psychology_of_.php

What Is Psychology? What Are The Branches Of Psychology? (n.d.). Retrieved from http://www.medicalnewstoday.com/articles/154874.php

Celebrity Suicides: An Unfortunate Trend - seoulbeats ... (n.d.). Retrieved from http://seoulbeats.com/2012/06/celebrity-suicides-an-unfortunate-trend/

Chapter 08

UNH Alumni Association - Home | University of New Hampshire. (n.d.). Retrieved from https://www.alumni.unh.edu/keep/stories/70/index.html

ROFESSIONAL ESPONSIBILITY OCIAL ONTRACT WITH UMANITY. (n.d.). Retrieved from http://www.ama-assn.org/resources/doc/ethics/decofprofessional.pdf

The Presidential Inauguration | St. Mary's University. (n.d.). Retrieved from http://www.stmarytx.edu/inauguration/index.php?site=inaugur ationAddress

Dáil Éireann - 20/Jun/2012 Other Questions - Garda Reserve. (n.d.). Retrieved from http://debates.oireachtas.ie/dail/2012/06/20/00015.asp

Book Reviews - The Color of Sunlight. (n.d.). Retrieved from http://www.tcosl.com/book-reviews.html

Miscellaneous Anthrax Articles - Part 2 - Analyzing The ... (n.d.). Retrieved from http://www.anthraxinvestigation.com/misc2.html

NeedleNecessities. (n.d.). Retrieved from
http://needlenecessities.blogspot.com/

78333294 the Secrets of a Lady Jenna Petersen. (n.d.). Retrieved
from http://www.scribd.com/doc/128139436/78333294-the-
Secrets-of-a-Lady-Jenna-Peterse
n

A pain like no other - Fiji Times Online. (n.d.). Retrieved from
http://www.fijitimes.com/story.aspx?id=231697

Chapter 09

Climate Change: What would Churchill Do? | Rooted. (n.d.).
Retrieved from
http://blogs.crikey.com.au/rooted/2010/06/30/climate-
change-what-would-churchill
-do/

colotube. (n.d.). Retrieved from
http://www.colotubeamplifiers.com/en/

Eight Keys to Life Hardiness and Resiliency | AsianWeek. (n.d.).
Retrieved from
http://www.asianweek.com/2009/09/03/preston-
ni%e2%80%99s-leadership-success-seri
es/

PearPC - PowerPC Architecture Emulator. (n.d.). Retrieved
from http://pearpc.sourceforge.net/

Personal Relationship & Lifestyle Questions | The Thinking ...
(n.d.). Retrieved from
http://thethinkingasexual.wordpress.com/2012/11/30/personal
-relationship-lifesty
le-questions/

Eight Keys to Life Hardiness and Resiliency | AsianWeek. (n.d.).
Retrieved from

http://www.asianweek.com/2009/09/03/preston-
ni%e2%80%99s-leadership-success-seri
es/

LETTERS FROM MOTHER MARY. (n.d.). Retrieved from
http://lettersfrommothermary.blogspot.com/

Chapter 10

A redeemed life | Just another WordPress.com weblog. (n.d.).
Retrieved from http://aredeemedlife.wordpress.com/

The Counselor Muses | Ponderings on Mental Health. (n.d.).
Retrieved from http://emilybryantphd.com/

La Plata UMC Pastor's Blog. (n.d.). Retrieved from
http://laplatapastors.blogspot.com/

Timberline - Port Angeles High School - Yes Kids, Santa ...
(n.d.). Retrieved from
http://my.hsj.org/Schools/Newspaper/tabid/100/view/frontp
age/schoolid/4266/artic
leid/565138/newspaperid/4481/Yes_Kids_Santa_Exists_contin
ued.aspx

Mental Illness and Exercise - NAMI: National Alliance on ...
(n.d.). Retrieved from
http://nami.org/Content/NavigationMenu/Hearts_and_Minds
/Exercise/Exercise.pdf

Where's Your Head At? - Welcome to Women's Running, the
UK's ... (n.d.). Retrieved from
http://www.womensrunninguk.co.uk/wheresyourheadat.obyx

Mind Guide to physical activity - MHUK - Mental Health In The
UK. (n.d.). Retrieved from
http://www.mentalhealthintheuk.co.uk/Mindguidetophysicalacti
v.pdf

Yoga Nidra Instructions | Art of Living India. (n.d.). Retrieved
from http://www.artofliving.org/in-en/yoga/health-and-
wellness/yoga-nidra

Samadhi | Free Music, Tour Dates, Photos, Videos. (n.d.).
Retrieved from http://www.myspace.com/samadhi2

igolu. (n.d.). Retrieved from http://igolu.com/

What is Self Awareness? How Self Aware are You? (n.d.).
Retrieved from http://www.selfcreation.com/self-
awareness/what-is-self-awareness.htm

Dive Deeper into Self Awareness by Questioning Your
Motivations. (n.d.). Retrieved from
http://www.selfcreation.com/self-awareness/question-why.htm

A First-Rate Madness : NPR. (n.d.). Retrieved from
http://www.npr.org/books/titles/139550918/a-first-rate-
madness-uncovering-the-li
nks-between-leadership-and-mental-illness

Mandala Oasis. (n.d.). Retrieved from
http://mandalaoasis.blogspot.com/

7rin_on_adoption | Recent Entries. (n.d.). Retrieved from
http://7rin-on-adoption.dreamwidth.org/

Development | Bellybuds. (n.d.). Retrieved from
http://www.bellybuds.com/?s=development

Lisa Belkin: Are We There Yet? The End Of Men, The Rise Of
Dads. (n.d.). Retrieved from
http://www.huffingtonpost.com/lisa-belkin/end-of-
men_b_1871501.html

Treatment Can Ease Lingering Trauma of Sept. 11 -
NYTimes.com. (n.d.). Retrieved from
http://www.nytimes.com/2001/11/20/science/treatment-can-

ease-lingering-trauma-of
-sept-11.html

A redeemed life | Just another WordPress.com weblog. (n.d.).
Retrieved from http://aredeemedlife.wordpress.com/

Chapter 11

The Ann Arbor Chronicle | PAC: Downtown Park, More Input
Needed. (n.d.). Retrieved from
http://annarborchronicle.com/2012/10/02/pac-downtown-
park-more-input-needed/

Encyclopedia entries starting with NIC - Who or What is ...
(n.d.). Retrieved from http://encycl.opentopia.com/N/NI/NIC

Spring Sights, Sounds, and Smells — Cold Climate Gardening.
(n.d.). Retrieved from
http://www.coldclimategardening.com/2007/05/13/sights-
sounds-and-smells-of-sprin
g/

March | 2011 | Elements Hyperlocal Journalism Photo-blog.
(n.d.). Retrieved from
http://pics4twitts.wordpress.com/2011/03/

Hawaii Photobooth - The Booth - Hawaii's Studio Style Photo
Booth. (n.d.). Retrieved from http://www.theboothhawaii.com/

Comments about 'Minutemen protest Salt Lake as 'sanctuary ...
(n.d.). Retrieved from
http://www.deseretnews.com/user/comments/705309370/Min
utemen-protest-Salt-Lake-a
s-sanctuary-for-illegal-immigrants.html

"If you're not rich, blame yourself" (Herman Cain vs ... (n.d.).
Retrieved from http://www.redletterchristians.org/if-youre-not-
rich-blame-yourself-herman-cain-
vs-john-wesley/

Mrs. Linklater's Guide to the Universe. (n.d.). Retrieved from http://mrslinklatersguidetotheuniverse.blogspot.com/

Youth - MSOCME. (n.d.). Retrieved from http://youth-msocme.blogspot.com/

WorldFest - LA's Largest Earth Day Festival! A solar-powered ... (n.d.). Retrieved from http://www.worldfestevents.com/

Chapter 12

India USA- some similarities - pezarkar's info site. adaniel ... (n.d.). Retrieved from http://adaniel.tripod.com/indiaamerica.htm

If Indians are so smart then why...? - Yahoo! Answers. (n.d.). Retrieved from http://answers.yahoo.com/question/index?qid=20090218044726AAx8qXj

In Praise of India: 30 Famous Quotations about India and Hinduism. (n.d.). Retrieved from http://hinduism.about.com/od/history/a/indiaquotes.htm

An Introduction to India - Geographia - World Travel ... (n.d.). Retrieved from http://www.geographia.com/india/

Stereotypes of South Asians - Wikipedia, the free encyclopedia. (n.d.). Retrieved from http://en.wikipedia.org/wiki/Stereotypes_of_South_Asians

Episode 4 Summary | The Story of India - About the Show | PBS. (n.d.). Retrieved from http://www.pbs.org/thestoryofindia/about/episode_summaries/4/

Episode Summaries | The Story of India - About the Show | PBS. (n.d.). Retrieved from

http://www.pbs.org/thestoryofindia/about/episode_summaries
/

What is the history of India? - Yahoo! Answers India. (n.d.).
Retrieved from
http://in.answers.yahoo.com/question/index?qid=20061007030
411AAyPCYL

How the Indo-Pakistani Border Came to Be - NYTimes.com.
(n.d.). Retrieved from
http://opinionator.blogs.nytimes.com/2012/07/03/peacocks-
at-sunset/

The Story of India | Watch Free Documentary Online. (n.d.).
Retrieved from http://topdocumentaryfilms.com/story-of-
india/

Japan used car bangladesh. (n.d.). Retrieved from
http://japanusedcarbangladesh.blogspot.com/

Delhi's Disappearing Night Sky - NYTimes.com. (n.d.).
Retrieved from
http://india.blogs.nytimes.com/2012/11/14/delhis-
disappearing-night-sky/

Protecting The Earth. (n.d.). Retrieved from
http://protectingtheearth.com/

ProjectDisaster » 2012 » June » 8. (n.d.). Retrieved from
http://projectdisaster.com/?m=20120608

Haq's Musings: New Index Finds Indians Poorer Than Africans
... (n.d.). Retrieved from
http://www.riazhaq.com/2010/07/new-index-finds-indians-
poorer-than.html

Never Mind Europe. Worry About India | Mercatus. (n.d.).
Retrieved from http://mercatus.org/expert_commentary/never-
mind-europe-worry-about-india

doakonsult. (n.d.). Retrieved from
http://doakonsult.wordpress.com/

Foreign media on coal scam and crony capitalism -
NDTVProfit.com. (n.d.). Retrieved from
http://profit.ndtv.com/news/economy/article-foreign-media-
on-coal-scam-and-crony
-capitalism-310883

India's electricity problems: An area of darkness | The ... (n.d.).
Retrieved from http://www.economist.com/node/21559977

India's Economy Slows, With Global Implications. (n.d.).
Retrieved from http://www.cnbc.com/id/47615018

Never Mind Europe. Worry About India | Mercatus. (n.d.).
Retrieved from http://mercatus.org/expert_commentary/never-
mind-europe-worry-about-india

Education Abroad | Quinnipiac University Connecticut. (n.d.).
Retrieved from
http://www.quinnipiac.edu/academics/multicultural-global-
education/education-abr
oad/helpful-links/

Registered Traveler Interoperability Consortium - News. (n.d.).
Retrieved from http://www.rtconsortium.org/news.cfm

US Struggles Anew to Ensure Safety as Gaps Are Revealed.
(n.d.). Retrieved from http://www.cnbc.com/id/34620831

Opinion: Too Many Contractors in Intelligence Community -
TIME. (n.d.). Retrieved from
http://www.time.com/time/nation/article/0,8599,2004876,00.h
tml

Airport security checks are vulnerable to fake boarding ... (n.d.).
Retrieved from http://articles.washingtonpost.com/2012-11-

03/world/35505464_1_bar-codes-securit
y-experts-security-researchers

India. (n.d.). Retrieved from
http://travel.state.gov/travel/cis_pa_tw/cis/cis_1139.html

US issues travel advisory for India during festive season ... (n.d.).
Retrieved from http://www.rediff.com/news/report/us-issues-
travel-advisory-for-india-during-fes
tive-season/20111020.htm

HowStuffWorks "How Airports Work". (n.d.). Retrieved from
http://science.howstuffworks.com/transport/flight/modern/air
port.htm

LAX: Behind the scenes at one of the world's busiest airports ...
(n.d.). Retrieved from
http://articles.latimes.com/2011/sep/30/travel/la-tr-lax-
20111002

MetroAirport.com. (n.d.). Retrieved from
http://www.metroairport.com/

What Type of Survivalist Are You? - Survival Cache — The ...
(n.d.). Retrieved from http://survivalcache.com/survivalist-
type/

Airports could ramp up service, cleanliness - Lifestyle - Ohio.
(n.d.). Retrieved from http://www.ohio.com/lifestyle/airports-
could-ramp-up-service-cleanliness-1.18427
4

One More Minute. (n.d.). Retrieved from http://one-more-
minute.blogspot.com/

Airport Essay - Example Essays.com - Over 80,000 essays, term
... (n.d.). Retrieved from
http://www.exampleessays.com/viewpaper/51874.html

Chapter 13

Find Your Way Through the Airport Maze, Phone in Hand ... (n.d.). Retrieved from http://article.wn.com/view/2012/07/18/Find_Your_Way_Through_the_Airport_Maze_Phone_in_Hand/

My Kind of Hong Kong | Hit the city with the beat of my heart ... (n.d.). Retrieved from http://maria0201.wordpress.com/

Amazon.com: The Kingdom of the Bears eBook: Michael Wallace ... (n.d.). Retrieved from http://www.amazon.com/The-Kingdom-Bears-ebook/dp/B004JU1JPM

Diabetic Meal Plans - Top 10 Tips for Achieving Best Personal ... (n.d.). Retrieved from http://franstips.com/diabetic-meal-plans-top-10-tips-for-achieving-best-personal-goal/

11 Worst U.S. Airports for Layovers | U.S. News Travel. (n.d.). Retrieved from http://travel.usnews.com/features/11_Worst_US_Airports_for_Layovers/

Atithi Devo Bhav - Wikipedia, the free encyclopedia. (n.d.). Retrieved from http://en.wikipedia.org/wiki/Atithi_Devo_Bhav

Air India B777-300ER business class - Business Traveller. (n.d.). Retrieved from http://www.businesstraveller.com/archive/2009/may-2009/tried-and-tested/air-indi a-b777-300er-business-class

Air India Boeing 787 Dreamliner Review - Business Line. (n.d.). Retrieved from http://www.thehindubusinessline.com/features/smartbuy/luxur y-and-fashion/air-ind ia-boeing-787-dreamliner-review/article3958042.ece

Airlines with the Most Beautiful Air Hostess in the World. (n.d.).
Retrieved from http://topics.dirwell.com/info/airlines-with-the-
most-beautiful-air-hostess-in-t
he-world.html

How do i choose between n ex i still love and the new guy in ...
(n.d.). Retrieved from
http://answers.yahoo.com/question/index?qid=2006100303080
1AAqkbwW

OC Jewish Experience. (n.d.). Retrieved from
http://ocjewishexperience.wordpress.com/

Dogs That Bite - How To Information | eHow.com. (n.d.).
Retrieved from http://www.ehow.com/dogs-that-bite/

Can turbulence cause a plane crash? - Slate Magazine. (n.d.).
Retrieved from
http://www.slate.com/articles/news_and_politics/explainer/20
12/06/can_turbulence
_cause_a_plane_crash_.html

BARNES & NOBLE | Beautiful Monster by Joely Skye |
Paperback. (n.d.). Retrieved from
http://www.barnesandnoble.com/w/beautiful-monster-joely-
skye/1008698351

Murtaza Bhutto - Wikipedia, the free encyclopedia. (n.d.).
Retrieved from http://en.wikipedia.org/wiki/Murtaza_Bhutto

A short primer on turbulence - Washington Post. (n.d.).
Retrieved from http://articles.washingtonpost.com/2012-11-
09/lifestyle/35503383_1_turbulence-fl
ight-attendant-planes

SIGNS & MIRACLES - Newsflashes about phenomena
worldwide. (n.d.). Retrieved from
http://themiraclespage.info/encounters/newsflashes.htm

Extinguishing the Fear at the Roots of Anxiety - NYTimes.com. (n.d.). Retrieved from http://www.nytimes.com/ref/health/healthguide/esn-anxiety-ess.html

Chapter 14

Planters' Punch - UFDC Home - All Collection Groups. (n.d.). Retrieved from http://ufdc.ufl.edu/AA00004645/00013

In Sermon And in Silence, Mother Teresa Is Celebrated - New ... (n.d.). Retrieved from http://www.nytimes.com/1997/09/09/nyregion/in-sermon-and-in-silence-mother-teres a-is-celebrated.html

If you're not rich, blame yourself' (Herman Cain vs ... (n.d.). Retrieved from http://www.redletterchristians.org/if-youre-not-rich-blame-yourself-herman-cain-vs-john-wesley/

Mrs. Linklater's Guide to the Universe. (n.d.). Retrieved from http://mrslinklatersguidetotheuniverse.blogspot.com/

Vulnerability is a risky business, mostly met by shame. How ... (n.d.). Retrieved from http://www.ted.com/conversations/10216/vulnerability_is_a_ri sky_busin.html

A coward dies a thousand deaths, a brave man dies but once. (n.d.). Retrieved from http://dorrys.com/coward-dies-death/

Historical Near-Death Experiences (Updated) | NHNE Pulse. (n.d.). Retrieved from http://nhne-pulse.org/historical-near-death-experiences/

HockeyBuzz.com - Andy Strickland - Toews and Oshie Moving On? (n.d.). Retrieved from http://www.hockeybuzz.com/blog.php?post_id=6624

Club Penguin Neighborhood: The First Club Penguin GameShow. (n.d.). Retrieved from http://clubpenguinneighborhood.blogspot.com/

Amazon.com: Pyle PLCM34WIR 3.5-Inch Monitor Wireless Back-Up ... (n.d.). Retrieved from http://www.amazon.com/Pyle-PLCM34WIR-3-5-Inch-Wireless-Rearview/dp/B003CN5NXG

Transponder (aviation) - Wikipedia, the free encyclopedia. (n.d.). Retrieved from http://en.wikipedia.org/wiki/Transponder_(aviation)

No Weather Complaints Today ("haboobs" hit Phoenix, Joplin EF ... (n.d.). Retrieved from http://www.startribune.com/blogs/125021754.html

When Disaster Threatens, Instinct Can Be a Pilot's Enemy ... (n.d.). Retrieved from http://www.post-gazette.com/stories/news/world/when-disaster-threatens-instinct-can-be-a-pilots-enemy-324813/

Eye On Oshkosh: January 2009. (n.d.). Retrieved from http://eyeonoshkosh.blogspot.com/2009_01_01_archive.html

Birdstrike in the Hudson | MetaFilter. (n.d.). Retrieved from http://www.metafilter.com/78307/Birdstrike-in-the-Hudson

This Miracle Brought to You by America's Unions | Emptywheel. (n.d.). Retrieved from http://emptywheel.firedoglake.com/2009/01/16/this-miracle-brought-to-you-by-amer icas-unions/

Police investigate murder-suicide in West Jordan | ksl.com. (n.d.). Retrieved from http://www.ksl.com/?nid=148&sid=8756531

illyoojeen » Comments | The Awl. (n.d.). Retrieved from
http://www.theawl.com/user/8244/illyoojeen

What You Need to Know About Air France Flight 447 - Adam
... (n.d.). Retrieved from
http://www.theatlanticwire.com/global/2011/05/what-you-
need-know-about-air-franc
e-flight-447/37360/

Unbearable: Delhi records worst summer in 33 years - Times Of
... (n.d.). Retrieved from
http://articles.timesofindia.indiatimes.com/2012-07-
03/delhi/32522483_1_maximum-
temperature-degree-national-climatic-data-center

How the hell did they find out about Secret Plan F451? (Reply ...
(n.d.). Retrieved from
http://www.democraticunderground.com/?com=view_post&fo
rum=1002&pid=1453165

Lynn Hagen - Shifters Of Mystery 3 - Jeremiah's Heart. (n.d.).
Retrieved from http://www.scribd.com/doc/117074760/Lynn-
Hagen-Shifters-Of-Mystery-3-Jeremiah-s-
Heart

Land and See: Infrared and 3-D Vision Systems Combine to
Help ... (n.d.). Retrieved from
http://www.scientificamerican.com/article.cfm?id=3d-pilot-
vision-air-safety

Question regarding late pick up by non custodial parent - VA.
(n.d.). Retrieved from http://forum.freeadvice.com/child-
custody-visitation-37/question-regarding-late-
pick-up-non-custodial-parent-va-579785.html

Hot Topics | Gossip | Hobbies | News | Sport. (n.d.).
Retrieved from http://andrekinadi.blogspot.com/

brand new. (n.d.). Retrieved from
http://garethkay.typepad.com/

Idaho Potato Commission. (n.d.). Retrieved from
http://www.idahopotato.com/?page=aristocrat_popup&is_pop
up=1&id=33

Full text of "Tales in Verse" - Internet Archive: Digital ... (n.d.).
Retrieved from
http://www.archive.org/stream/talesinverse00howigoog/talesin
verse00howigoog_djvu
.txt

Chapter - 15

VERSIONS OF HUMAN NATURE. (n.d.). Retrieved from
http://isik.zrc-
sazu.si/doc2009/kpms/ORIGINS_OF_THE_SOCIAL_BRAI
N-Allan_Young.pdf

S v Marais (CA&R715/2004) [2008] ZAECHC 112; 2009 (1)
SACR ... (n.d.). Retrieved from
http://www.saflii.org/za/cases/ZAECHC/2008/112.html

Katherine Dolgy Ludwig | The Artist Project 2013. (n.d.).
Retrieved from
http://www.theartistprojecttoronto.com/gp_artists/katherine-
dolgy-ludwig/

Ask Alec Baldwin: Ignore flight attendants at your peril ... (n.d.).
Retrieved from http://travel.usatoday.com/flights/story/2011-
12-09/Ask-Alec-Baldwin-Ignore-flig
ht-attendants-at-your-peril/51771362/1

U.S. Bank | FlexPerks Traveler Photo Contest. (n.d.). Retrieved
from http://flexperkstraveler.usbank.com/

BBC - History : British History Timeline. (n.d.). Retrieved from
http://www.bbc.co.uk/history/british/timeline/worldwars_time
line_noflash.shtml

United makes emergency landing at Newark Liberty Intl Airport
... (n.d.). Retrieved from
http://www.nowpublic.com/world/united-makes-emergency-
landing-newark-liberty-int
l-airport

Strong Life Quote - Answer The Call - Daily Inspirational ...
(n.d.). Retrieved from http://www.daily-inspirational-
quotes.net/daily-quotes-05092011.html

Hudson Landing An Engineering Miracle, Pilot Says : NPR.
(n.d.). Retrieved from
http://www.npr.org/templates/story/story.php?storyId=12035
5655

A Tense Landing at Newark Airport | 4 Business World. (n.d.).
Retrieved from http://4businessworld.info/blog/12/a-tense-
landing-at-newark-airport/

Mera Joota Hai Japani - Wikipedia, the free encyclopedia. (n.d.).
Retrieved from
http://en.wikipedia.org/wiki/Mera_Joota_Hai_Japani

Chapter 16

Applications to Use a Public Road for Activities (Sport and ...
(n.d.). Retrieved from
http://www.westerncape.gov.za/eng/directories/services/11598
/5123

Travel - Search for 'byline:By BARRY BEARAK' - The New
York Times. (n.d.). Retrieved from
http://travel.nytimes.com/gst/travel/travsearch.html?term=byli
ne%3ABy%20BARRY%20
BEARAK

Flights from London, United Kingdon to Delhi, India? - Yahoo
... (n.d.). Retrieved from
http://answers.yahoo.com/question/index?qid=2008040807433
8AArMi6e

STROLLING THROUGH THE PARK; NEW DELHI - New
York Times. (n.d.). Retrieved from
http://www.nytimes.com/1992/03/01/magazine/strolling-
through-the-park-new-delhi.
html

STROLLING THROUGH THE PARK; NEW DELHI - New
York Times. (n.d.). Retrieved from
http://www.nytimes.com/1992/03/01/magazine/strolling-
through-the-park-new-delhi.
html

The great Indian kiss - Yahoo! News India. (n.d.). Retrieved
from http://in.news.yahoo.com/great-indian-kiss-
183000597.html

WHAT'S DOING IN; Delhi - New York Times. (n.d.).
Retrieved from
http://www.nytimes.com/2003/11/30/travel/what-s-doing-in-
delhi.html

Confessions of a Gay Travel Agent | Gay and Lesbian Journeys
... (n.d.). Retrieved from http://outjourneys.wordpress.com/

WHAT'S DOING IN; New Delhi - New York Times. (n.d.).
Retrieved from
http://www.nytimes.com/1998/10/18/travel/what-s-doing-in-
new-delhi.html

WHAT'S DOING IN; Delhi - New York Times. (n.d.).
Retrieved from
http://www.nytimes.com/2003/11/30/travel/what-s-doing-in-
delhi.html

India Photos -- National Geographic. (n.d.). Retrieved from http://travel.nationalgeographic.com/travel/countries/india-photos/

Mango festival, Pitampura - YouTube. (n.d.). Retrieved from http://www.youtube.com/watch?v=3yokWnpgENk

Golden Triangle India Tour, Delhi Agra Sightseeing Tours ... (n.d.). Retrieved from http://shinegoldtoursindia.com/

Rajasthan | Boundless Journeys Blog - Adventure Tours ... (n.d.). Retrieved from http://blog.boundlessjourneys.com/tag/rajasthan/

luísa alpalhão. (n.d.). Retrieved from http://luisaalpalhao.blogspot.com/

North to Ladakh, on a High-Altitude Adventure - New York Times. (n.d.). Retrieved from http://www.nytimes.com/1999/02/28/magazine/north-to-ladakh-on-a-high-altitude-ad venture.html

Travel | Traveling in luxury high in the Himalayas | Seattle ... (n.d.). Retrieved from http://seattletimes.com/html/travel/2014098651_webladakh01. html

Full text of "Journal". (n.d.). Retrieved from http://tvarchive2.archive.org/stream/journalmanch29mancuoft /journalmanch29mancuo ft_djvu.txt

Wanderer above the Sea of Fog - Wikipedia, the free encyclopedia. (n.d.). Retrieved from http://en.wikipedia.org/wiki/Wanderer_above_the_Sea_of_Fog

Cat ♥ ♥ on Myspace. (n.d.). Retrieved from http://www.myspace.com/devil_catt13#!

A Silk Road Adoption Story. (n.d.). Retrieved from
http://www.silkroadstory.blogspot.com/

Mastery to take over Hardy Williams Charter | Philadelphia ...
(n.d.). Retrieved from
http://thenotebook.org/blog/113436/mastery-take-over-hardy-
williams-charter

Villages Without Doctors - NYTimes.com - Opinion ... (n.d.).
Retrieved from
http://opinionator.blogs.nytimes.com/2011/02/14/villages-
without-doctors/

BARNES & NOBLE | The Woman in White by Wilkie Collins
| NOOK ... (n.d.). Retrieved from
http://www.barnesandnoble.com/w/woman-in-white-wilkie-
collins/1001834504?ean=294
0026243396

'Falling Skies' 'Shall We Gather at the River': Tick tick ... (n.d.).
Retrieved from http://www.examiner.com/article/falling-skies-
shall-we-gather-at-the-river-tick-
tick-boom

A redeemed life | Just another WordPress.com weblog. (n.d.).
Retrieved from http://aredeemedlife.wordpress.com/

ABOUT THE AUTHOR

Nand Arora is a former business executive for various Fortune 500 companies and founder of East and West Film Productions LLC and other businesses. He plans to produce and direct a Hindi film based on this novel. He also teaches business and economics courses at graduate and undergraduate level.

24394868R20119

Made in the USA
Charleston, SC
24 November 2013